To Kathryn:
It was great to meet you! So glad you liked my book. Thanks for The nice review.

The Strange Tale of Ben Beesley

by

Matt McNeil

Best wishes,

D1367656

For my children, Waverly & Oliver,
my friends, Mackenzie, Blair, Jessie, Tom & Sophie,
and all the other beautiful children
afflicted with MPS III.

Contents

The Strange Tale of Ben Beesley

CHAPTER ONE
WISHES

Two flies lay on the side of a hill gazing up at the night sky. "Do you think we'll see any shooting stars tonight?" Oliver asked his older sister, Waverly.

"I'm sure we'll see some," she answered, pulling at a blade of grass. "Could be our lucky night."

"What are you going to wish for?" he asked.

"If I tell you, it won't come true."

"That's just an old fly's tale. You actually make your wish more powerful if you share it with someone."

"You made that up, but if you must know, I'm going to wish ... that we come home with something special from the city tomorrow."

Because Waverly and Oliver were flies, and common house flies at that, they were required to live near the fly-city of Diterra. Equally full of filth and life, it was a rowdy, dangerous place, but a familiar one; they had been going to the market there since they were very young. From their hill on that fall night, Diterra looked deceptively peaceful sitting on the far western edge of a long-neglected garden.

To a bug, the garden was enormous and contained incredibly diverse landscapes, from rocky mountains and barren, dusty plains, to vast murky lakes and overgrown forests. From one end of the garden to the other there was one constant: every plant was on the verge of dying. Whatever the cause, whether choking weeds, nutrient-depleted soil, reluctant rains, or the scorching sun, the result was the same—a shabby collection of grayish plants struggling to stay alive.

"Remember when we found Pupa hiding behind an avocado pit at the market?" asked Oliver. Pupa, a small white creature with six stubby legs, was asleep, curled up in front of the entrance to a hollowed out apple they used for shelter.

"And how Mom lured him out, then pretended like Pupa found us so Dad would feel sorry for him?"

"Maybe you'll come home with another Pupa."

"I think one is plenty." Just then, the first shooting star of the night streaked across the sky. "There it is," Waverly declared, covering her eyes. A moment later, she added, "Made my wish."

"Good one," said Oliver as he pushed the tip of his left antenna out of his eye.

Each of these flies had short and slender antennae sprouting up from behind a pair of red, bulging eyes on the top of their heads. The straw-shaped tongues hidden inside their small mouths resembled an elephant's trunk when they extended it to eat their food. Both had six legs, three on each side of their body. Their wings would have been completely transparent if not for the thin veins laced throughout. Black hairs dotted their plump bodies, although Waverly was less round than Oliver, whose legs were also a bit stubby.

"What's your wish going to be?" asked Waverly.

"I don't know if I should tell you," he said.

"Oh, come on."

"I'm going to wish I was a bee."

"Again with the bees. You're getting a little crazy with the bee thing."

"What's wrong with liking bees?"

"What's wrong with being a fly?"

"Nothing, I guess, it's just that bees are so cool. You told me yourself everything was better when they were still here. We could use some bees again, so why not me?"

"Because you're a fly, Oliver," Waverly reminded him. "You will always be a fly."

"Hey, it's my wish." After a few silent moments, another shooting star ripped through the sky. Oliver lowered his head and concentrated. Looking up, he said, "Now it's officially my wish."

"Great," she said, "if you do turn into a bee, bring me some honey."

"I might sting you instead." They sat quietly until Oliver explained the rules for making a "together wish" as he made them up: "When a shooting star appears, two bugs make the same wish at the same time on the same star, and, this is the tricky part, both have to believe it will come true. If you do that, the wish is twice as likely to come true."

"What should we wish for?" asked Waverly.

"That Mom and Dad come back," he blurted out. When their parents disappeared, Waverly and Oliver searched every-

5

where but found no trace of them. Almost all of the bugs they talked with told them they hadn't seen anything. Diterra was like that—nobody saw anything even when they did. A few bugs did tell them of a rumor their parents were last seen with a pair of spiders, but Waverly and Oliver never learned what really happened to them.

"You know that won't ever happen, right?"

"It could if you believed it would."

"They're gone, Oliver. Let's pick something we can both believe in."

He thought for a moment. Turning to Waverly he whispered as though what he had to say was too dangerous to be spoken aloud. "Then let's wish the spiders go away."

Spiders were everywhere in the garden, though seldom seen as they preferred to lurk in the shadows. The undisputed king of the spiders was Ramsay, who ruled from a forbidding beehive on the opposite side of the garden from Diterra. Ramsay maintained control by making rules that were impossible to keep, then harshly punishing any rule-breakers. Working together was banned because Ramsay feared the bugs would rebel if they were allowed to collaborate. There was no eating in the company of others. Laughing out loud was strictly prohibited. The list went on and on. The other spiders bowed down to Ramsay and lived to enforce his rules. Every bug that ever lived would eventually run afoul of those rules, and the consequences were dire.

Waverly looked around to see if they were being watched. Confident they were alone, she lay back down and whispered, "Now that's a wish I can believe in."

Seconds later, they spotted another shooting star and made their together wish. Instead of disappearing from the sky, the tail of the star grew longer and more brilliant. At first, they thought it good luck to have wished on such a magnificent star. Soon they realized the star was getting bigger because it was coming right at them. They quickly went from awe-struck to terrified.

They held their breath as it passed by so closely it singed the hair on their head and blew their antennae into their faces. When it was directly overhead, time rolled forward in slow motion. What they saw did not look like a shooting star. In the middle of the streaking light, they saw a small black blur and two bulging red eyes. *If anything,* thought Waverly, *it looked like a fly.* Seconds after it passed over them, whatever-it-was landed with a thud in the middle of Diterra.

Waverly and Oliver looked at each other in astonishment. The same thought crossed both their minds: What if the spiders heard their rule-breaking wish? Surely, not even Ramsay was powerful enough to threaten them with a shooting star. Or was he? Not knowing filled them with such dread they would have preferred that the whatever-it-was landed *on* them than incur the wrath of Ramsay for their defiant wish-making.

The thought they might have been found out brought about such terror they rushed down the hill and into their house. Pupa woke as they leapt over him to get through the doorway. He yawned, stretched, and casually followed them inside. Waverly and Oliver hid under old leaves and blades of grass and pretended to sleep even as their hearts pounded and they struggled to catch their breath. Neither spoke a word the rest of the night, fearing they had said too much already.

***

Far away from Diterra, on the eastern edge of the garden, a massive beehive nestled into the side of a mountain. Perched atop the Hive sat a large spider with red glowing eyes. He was lean, and his long legs came to spear-like points at the tips. Black fur covered his whole body, except for a crown-shaped patch of brown flesh in the middle of his back where no hair grew at all. Two yellowing fangs jutted out the corners of his razor-toothed mouth.

The spider was Ramsay, and the Hive on the lonely mountain was his castle. He had been keeping a watchful eye on his garden, when the black speck shot across the sky. Upon seeing it land, he stood on his back four legs and looked toward Diterra. After careful inspection, he lowered himself and nervously tapped his forelegs together in front of his face as he thought. He pondered for a few moments, then his eyes widened, and he scurried down the side of the Hive and disappeared within.

Except for the sound of a gusting wind, the garden was perfectly silent at that moment. No one knew it yet, but the days that followed would bring fantastic upheaval. Everything in the garden was about to change.

But first, a small mosquito emerged from the Hive and filled the night with an irritating buzzing sound as he flew toward Diterra.

CHAPTER TWO
DITERRA

Waverly and Oliver did not sleep all night for fear the spiders had found them out. Morning brought with it the hope they might be all right after all. But when dawn broke, and they were able to relax at last, they had no choice but to get up.

Since they never slept, they didn't have to wonder if they had dreamt the shooting star crashing into Diterra. They knew with certainty what they had seen was real, and it made them curious. *What was that thing? Where did it land? Why had it come to the garden?* But Diterra was not the kind of place where questions were welcome. Besides, snooping would only draw attention, and after their sleepless night, attention was the last thing they wanted. Best just to forget it they decided.

Fortunately, it was market day, and a trip into Diterra would be the perfect cure for their lingering nervousness. One of the good fortunes in the lives of these two flies was the small fruit tree next to their home that littered the ground with rotting apples. During daylight hours, they foraged through the fallen fruit, keeping some for themselves and gathering the rest to trade. With autumn nearly over, the garden's insects were preparing themselves for a long slog through the bleak months ahead. In Diterra, these flies could exchange their bits of apple for food and other supplies needed to make it through to spring.

To get their merchandise to the city's market, Waverly and Oliver used a cart their parents had made out of a pine cone long ago. They stuffed bits of apple in between the scales of the cone until it was crammed full. Four round acorns attached underneath allowed the cart to roll easily even when filled to capacity. Twigs tied along the sides made perfect handles for two little flies. On the back side of the cart, above the wheels and below the handles, hung a net they used for extra storage.

Always sad to lose their company for the day, Pupa tried to follow Waverly and Oliver as they set off for Diterra. He relented only when Oliver got stern with him, at which point he retreated to their yard. They got an early start, heading down the hill toward the road that led to Diterra as the sun was rising.

There were only two other homes between the Beesley's house and the road. The nearest neighbor, Mrs. Galway, was a widowed fly who talked only to herself. Everyone else she yelled at. On this morning, Mrs. Galway sounded crankier than usual. "You kids keep that cart out of my yard!" she screamed from inside her run-down house.

"We're not even near her yard," muttered Oliver under his breath. "Mean old dragon fly."

"No name calling." Then Waverly called out, "Good morning, Mrs. Galway. Don't worry, we're not in your yard. We're on the path."

"Why are you so nice to that old coot?"

"Mom always said just because she's not nice to us doesn't mean we can't be nice to her." Oliver moved his lips in sync with Waverly's as she finished her sentence. "Oh, knock it off," she said, giving her brother a shove.

Beyond Mrs. Galway's place was the Lockwood residence. As the only other kids in the neighborhood, Todd and Chip Lockwood had been Waverly and Oliver's sole playmates. Over the years, though, they played less and less, and if not for the times they fought, they would barely interact at all. Just beyond the Lockwood house, Waverly and Oliver took a right turn onto a dusty road that led to the city.

They had been on the road nearly twenty minutes when a squat, pug-faced creature about the same size as Pupa howled at them. A hairy fly, who was easily twice the size of both the Beesley kids, stumbled out of a nearby hut, yelled "Be quiet!" and walloped the creature with a long stick. He struck the animal a few more times as Waverly and Oliver looked on in horror. The animal fell onto its side and whimpered. Oliver, imagining his beloved Pupa suffering the same harsh treatment, had seen enough. When the fly raised the stick over his head yet again, Oliver hollered, "Why don't you pick on someone your own size?"

The fly pointed the stick at them and slurred, "Mind your own business, or you'll be next, pee wee." While the fly was threatening Oliver, the creature scrambled around to the back of the hut. The fly stumbled after him, falling to the ground. He lay where he fell, shouting at Waverly and Oliver, but not even trying to get up. They kept their distance as they walked by him.

"That was scary," said Waverly. "I'm a little nervous to walk home this way."

"He won't even remember it tonight," said Oliver.

Waverly said, "Hope so, but I think he missed your point about picking on someone his own size ... pee wee."

Encounters such as these—all too typical of a day in Diterra—were a sure sign they were getting closer to the city. There were plenty of other signs too. Houses became huts, and the huts turned to hovels, creeping closer together until it was impossible to tell where one ended and the other began. What appeared to be stately structures from a distance turned out to be nothing more than piles of trash packed together with globs of mud, many of which looked ready to fall over at any moment. In the light of day there was no hiding the abundant filth. Garbage lined every street, piled so high it was impossible to tell where the rubbish heap ended and the buildings began.

The city's streets were rough. Bugs bumped and pushed, snarled and shoved. Courtesy had no meaning, and "pardon me" garnered only confused looks. Up close, Diterra—this crowded, bustling, and unpleasant city—was a dangerous place. As they entered the city that morning, Waverly and Oliver passed under a sign which read, "Diterra: Every Fly For Himself."

A gravelly-voiced fly hiding in an alley asked them if they wanted to buy some maggots as he looked every direction but theirs. They walked on by. Passing an apartment building, they heard shouting and the sounds of fighting getting louder. Suddenly, the front door flew open and two flies, each with their hands around the other's neck, tumbled out onto the street. They traded punches as more flies flooded out of the building to watch. Waverly and Oliver kept going.

On the next block, they saw a fly sitting behind a table with three leaves on it. He hid a stone under one of the leaves and asked if anyone wanted to guess which leaf it was under. A bug laid down some money and pointed to the leaf in the middle. Before his guess could be proved right or wrong, a strong wind blew all the leaves away revealing no stones under any of them. The fly running the game scooped up the money and took off down the street, with an angry crowd following close behind. A few moments later a greenish liquid fell from a tall building and landed on the head of a bug who stood only a few inches from Waverly. The Beesleys weren't sure what it was but knew it was disgusting. They picked up their pace, not wanting to give the flies above them a chance to reload.

They had nearly made it to the center of Diterra when a wobbly-eyed bug came up to them carrying a case. He held it out and popped it open as he said, "For the lady, I've got authentic Chanel Number Fly or a Roach handbag. Believe me, you'll get it way cheaper here than you will in that market. And sir, I did not forget you. I'm also an exclusive distributor for Timmy Earwigger." Waverly and Oliver politely declined. The fly called them a few unpleasant names before wandering off to bother somebody else.

At last, they made it to the market at the center of the city. In an hour or two it would be swarmed with vendors selling all sorts of things and shoppers eager to find bargains. As Waverly and Oliver had learned over the years, securing a good location was the difference between a successful trading day and a flop. Show up late and they'd get stuck in the back where too few shoppers passed or on the perimeter where, inevitably, much of a seller's merchandise got stolen. The best spots were in the middle of the market, toward the front. The upside of their sleepless night was it gave them an early start and with it, a chance at a good space for trading. They picked their spot and headed toward it.

As they rushed through the rapidly growing crowd of vendors, they heard a voice in a thick accent call out, "Look who's here—it's the Beesley kids."

That friendly voice brought smiles to their faces. "Mr. Mosca!" they called back.

"How many times do I have to tell you, call me Guido."

"Ok, Mr. Guido," said Waverly while giving him a quick hug.

After setting down the cart, Oliver gave a hug and asked, "What are you selling today, Mr. Guido?"

Waverly and Oliver had known Guido Mosca since they first started coming to the market and always marveled that he never seemed to sell the same product twice. From sour oranges to rancid meat, housewares to jewelry, most bugs had a specialty, and they sold the same thing every single day, no matter what. Mr. Mosca, however, sold a bit of everything over the years and how he did it remained a mystery.

"Oliver, my boy, today I've got the tastiest nuts in this entire market. I got almonds, pistachios, macadamia. And for you, I've got a free sample. And you can't refuse it—your parents were good friends to me."

Oliver took the nuts just as a potential customer approached Mr. Mosca to haggle over prices. With Mr. Mosca busy, Waverly and Oliver turned their attention to their neighbor on the other side. "What are you selling?" asked Oliver.

Glaring at Oliver, a fly with a hunched back answered, "Poop-pourri. No samples." Her voice was monotone and scratchy.

"Shucks. My loss," said Oliver, as he gave Waverly a wink. The gruff fly turned her back on them. They allowed that exchange to be both the beginning and the end of their conversation with Ms. Pourri (as they called her) and arranged their space so they could sell their apples right off their cart.

Market days started slowly, but by mid-morning a crush of flies standing wing to wing pushed their way through the aisles.

Together, Waverly and Oliver managed their improvised shop. They attracted customers, made flattering small talk, sealed deals, and did whatever else needed to be done to make their day a success. Sometimes they sold their apples for money, but more often they bartered them for other goods. The day's receipts included a raspberry, half a radish, a garland made out of bluebell flowers, and a shell filled with indigo dye.

About an hour before dusk, the crowd thinned considerably. Waverly told Oliver she wanted to browse the market to pick up things they needed for home and maybe find a special treat of her own.

"That's great," replied Oliver. "You can do that after I pee. I haven't gone all day."

"But the stores might close soon. Some vendors are already packing up. If I don't go now, I could miss my chance to buy our things," she reasoned.

"Ok, go look," answered Oliver. "But I really have to go, so don't take forever."

Waverly rushed into the aisles, turning back over her shoulder to remind Oliver, "Remember, don't go anywhere until I come back."

"You don't have to tell me that. Just hurry up!" She was already too far away to hear.

Out in the market as a shopper, Waverly searched for the best deals and was careful not to look too eager to buy. While this approach saved money, it cost her time. After circling all the shops once, she picked up some items they needed around the house, carefully avoiding the sellers who had tried to rip her off in the past.

She knew she had to get back to relieve Oliver so he could relieve himself, but she wanted to take one last look to see if she could find a special sort of something that changes a normal day out into something more memorable—the sort of thing she had wished for the night before.

Remembering a vendor selling dolls that caught her eye earlier, she circled back around to his shop to take a closer look. Waverly never had a doll before. She was old enough to feel like she had always wanted one and young enough to still want it. She was holding an orange-haired doll she adored in one hand and considering the asking price when she noticed him for the first time. A young fly, about her age, was climbing up out of a mound of trash.

In Diterra, there was nothing unusual about seeing a fly climb in, around, through, or out of garbage. However, there was something about the way this particular fly did it that caught her attention. Normally, a fly coming out of a rubbish heap would look as though he had been buried in it, with pieces of trash shifting around him whenever he moved. But this fly looked more like he was climbing up onto a cliff after scaling the side of a mountain. The whole scene made her curious and she wanted to take a closer look. She handed the doll back to the vendor and said, "I might be back."

Walking around the doll seller's stall, she watched the mysterious fly totter on the trash pile before he tumbled down to the street. He got back on his feet but stumbled around like he had lost his sense of balance. He moved with the uncertainty of one blinded by the sunlight after coming out of a darkened room. His arms were extended, groping at the air as he walked. The bugs in the area kept their distance from him.

As Waverly drew closer, she could more clearly see the hole he climbed out of. To her surprise, it was fly-shaped—a fly body, two wings, and six legs bent in every which direction—cut into the trash heap with cookie-cutter precision. This only made her more curious. She flew up to look into the hole. Not only did it go all the way to the bottom of the trash pile, to her amazement the hole went at least two feet into the ground. *How in the world did he make this hole?* she thought. Suddenly Waverly recalled the shooting star from the night before. *No way! That's not possible.*

When she looked back at the fly staggering in the street, she also saw two spiders slink out of a dark alley and step right in front of him. The fly ran right into the rear end of one of the spiders and was knocked even more off balance than he already was. Attempting to catch himself, he reached out and grabbed a clump of one of the spider's hair.

The spider, reacting with lethal speed, spun around, wrapped his hands over the fly's neck, yanked him off the ground, and pinned him to the nearest wall. Pushing his face up next to the fly's, the spider whispered through clenched teeth, "I hope you're ready to have a very bad day."

How Waverly wished she would have gotten to this fly before the spiders had.

CHAPTER THREE
OUR BROTHER BEN

The strange fly's feet swung back and forth as he dangled in midair. His face bore a dazed expression that allowed him to look right at the spider without seeming to notice him. He said nothing, made no noise, not even a whimper.

"You really shouldn't have done that, mate," said the other spider. "My pal Ug here, he don't got much patience with you flies."

"Did you really think you could attack me, and we'd let you walk away?" growled Ug, shifting his grip on the fly's neck. The fly did not answer.

"Now why don't you tell your pal Dap who put you up to it?" The spiders were always on the lookout for signs of conspiracies, convinced some bug, somewhere, was plotting a rebellion. The fly turned his blank stare in Dap's direction but remained silent.

"Hal-looo," said Dap, waving his hand in front of the fly's face. "Nothing, huh? Even I'm losing patience with you now, mate."

Ug pulled the fly away from the wall only to slam him back against it. "Are you part of a gang?" he hissed. Ug slammed him again. "Or are you just crazy?" Bam! Once more, into the wall. "Answer me!"

Waverly stood motionless on the trash heap, watching the spiders' rough treatment of the fly. She wished desperately he would say or do anything to try to save himself.

"Tell you what," interrupted Dap. Ug calmed slightly as his companion spoke. "You've got until the count of three to start explaining yourself or it's off to the Dung Heap with you. Understood?"

The fly looked down, appearing to realize for the first time his feet weren't on the ground.

"One," said Dap.

The fly looked between the spiders, toward the hole he had climbed out of. For a second his gaze rested on Waverly, and his eyes flashed with recognition. Waverly felt he was looking to her for help.

"Two."

The fly looked back at the spiders and opened his mouth as though getting ready to speak, yet still said nothing.

"Thr ..."

"STOP!" screamed Waverly in such a loud voice that everyone around her froze in place. "Stop! Don't hurt him."

In Diterra, flies avoided spiders at all costs and fervently hoped spiders would leave them alone in return. There was an unwritten rule that flies did nothing to draw attention to themselves when spiders were present. If a spider took an interest in a fly, two things were certain: the encounter *never* ended well for the fly, and the city motto, "every fly for himself," applied doubly.

But Waverly had broken the rule. She couldn't leave this fly to fend for himself. Something irresistible drew her to him. Nevertheless, Waverly shocked even herself, for she not only talked to a spider, she just *yelled* at two of them.

When Waverly felt the spiders' gaze resting upon her like a weight, her thoughts shifted from *what have I done?* to *what am I going to do now?* It occurred to her they might want an explanation for why she had yelled at them. If she didn't think of something soon—that is, something other than "I didn't want to you to hurt him because that's all you spiders seem to know how to do"—she would join this fly on his way to the Dung Heap.

She slowly climbed rather than flew down from the mound of garbage, buying time to think of something to say. With every step she focused more and more on the fact she had not yet thought of anything. When only a few inches separated her and the spiders, she panicked, and her mind went completely blank. Her hands trembled. Her legs wobbled. Although her mind had not yet supplied her with the words to utter, she opened her mouth to speak. When nothing came out, she was certain she would soon experience the spiders' wrath. Instead, at that very moment, Oliver came tearing around the corner running as fast as his legs could carry him.

"Waverly!" he shouted. "Where have you been? I told you I had to ... go." Oliver stopped abruptly when he realized Waverly was standing in the shadows of two menacing spiders. That his sister was evidently in trouble so terrified him that he lost control and went where he stood. He was now terrified and embarrassed. But Oliver's arrival gave Waverly the idea she had been searching for.

"Thank ... thank goodness you f-found our brother," she spit out. She knew if she sounded scared, the spiders wouldn't be convinced. Taking a deep breath, she collected herself for a better performance. "We've been worried sick about him. He wandered off, and we didn't know where he went."

Ug lowered the fly to the ground as she talked.

"Who are you?" asked Dap.

"I'm Waverly, and this is Oliver, sir. I'm sorry to be so forward, but we wanted to thank you for finding our brother."

Ug loosened his grip. Dap asked, "What's your brother's name?" pointing to the fly, who was relieved to have his neck freed of Ug's hands.

"That's our brother ... Ben," said Oliver, saying the first name that popped into his head. He could only wonder how Waverly got into this situation, but he was not going to wait for an explanation before he helped her get out of it.

"Your brother, Ben, eh? I guess he does look a bit like the both of you," Dap muttered. "But then again, all you flies look alike."

"It's hard to tell us apart. Guess that's a good reason for us to keep a closer eye on him," said Oliver.

"We can take him from here. He won't bother you again," said Waverly as she reached for the fly's hand.

Ug batted her hand away. She flinched and feared the spiders hadn't believed their story. "Hold on," Ug said. "He's defective. We can send him to the Dung Heap for that."

Under Ramsay's rules a "defective" bug—one whose brain or body did not work properly in some respect—could be sent to the Dung Heap for being a burden on the garden, whether he was or not. Waverly had no idea if Ben's brain worked correctly, but she wasn't going to let him get cast aside simply because it didn't.

"Oh, he's not defective," said Waverly, regrouping her confidence. "He hit his head real hard the other day, and he's been a little off since. But he should be back to normal soon."

"Oh, yeah," stated Ug. "Did a doctor tell you that, or are you just hoping for the best? Cause he don't look the least bit normal to me."

"Don't be so hard on 'em Ug. Let's let 'em go."

"Let 'em go? I don't think these two have ever seen this one before!"

"Let's ask the quiet one then," offered Dap. "If he knows 'em, we let 'em go. If not, then they all go to the Dung Heap." Leaning close to Ben he asked, "What do you say Ben? You know these two, do you?"

Ben raised his head, looked right at Dap, and in a weak voice uttered, "Home."

Waverly and Oliver were relieved at Ben's timing, It would be the only thing they heard him say all night, but it was enough.

"Fine," said Dap, "take him. But if any of you even look at a spider again, that'll be it for you. Now get out of here!"

Oliver and Waverly took Ben from the spiders right before he passed out and his head sunk into his chest. They draped his arms over their shoulders and their legs quivered as they walked back to their cart. At that moment, Waverly started to comprehend just how dangerous a game she had played. She risked her life for a fly she had never seen before. Although she knew she had done the right thing, she promised herself she would never be so impulsive again.

Behind them, they heard the spiders' voices drifting away. "I can't believe you let them go," Ug said. "We had more than enough to take in all three of them."

"They're just kids," countered Dap. "Why can't we give 'em a little break every now and then?"

"Because we're not supposed to. We're supposed to break bugs who break the law."

"It just didn't feel right," said Dap. "It was an accident."

Once Waverly and Oliver could no longer hear the spiders, they exhaled deeply and quickened their step, not fully trusting their luck or the spiders' uncharacteristic leniency. They hurried past the vendors who had already packed up and were headed for home in the fading light of the setting sun.

Another surprise awaited them back at their cart. Almost everything they traded for that day and every bit of apple they brought with them was gone. Except for a few items they had packed in the net underneath, the cart had been completely looted. Oliver had asked Mr. Mosca to keep an eye on their goods until he came back, but Mr. Mosca was nowhere to be found.

Overhearing the young flies wondering what had happened to Mr. Mosca and their apples, Ms. Pourri announced, "He's gone and he took your stuff." Her voice tinged with pleasure as she delivered the bad news.

"Why would Mr. Mosca do a thing like that?" asked Oliver. "He's our friend."

"No such thing as a friend in Diterra," coughed Ms. Pourri. "At least now you know how he's able to sell something different every time he comes. That's why I never take my eyes off that cockroach."

"Forget it, Oliver," whispered Waverly. "We just need to get out of here."

Waverly was right; they had no time to nurse any grievances. The anger and disappointment they felt seemed trivial in light of what they had been through. They had escaped with their lives, but only just. The only thing that mattered now was getting home.

They gently laid Ben face down on their cart with his body hugging the pine cone and his head near the handles. This stranger, for whom they risked so much, about whom they knew so little, was coming home with them, whether he liked it or not.

CHAPTER FOUR
ESCAPE FROM DITERRA

As Waverly and Oliver prepared to leave the city, the mosquito sent from Ramsay's Hive breezed into Diterra. He traveled through the market, passing over the Beesleys before reaching the two tallest buildings in the city. Between them, suspended in midair, a beady-eyed, brown spider sat on an expansive web. The mosquito flew straight to the web, stopping a few inches from the spider whose fangs poked out of his mouth and rested against his lower lip.

"Nothy, old boy! How the filth are you?" said the mosquito, hovering in place.

Noth was the commander of Ramsay's spiders in Diterra. "What do you want, Floyd?" he replied with contempt.

"Why so grumpy?" asked Floyd, turning over to hover upside down. "Did my arresting good looks remind you how ugly you are? I know it's hard, but don't hate me for being beautiful. Besides, you should be excited to see me. I just might save your skin."

"How do you figure?" Noth wanted nothing more than to fill Floyd with venom but reminded himself the mosquito was Ramsay's personal messenger.

"Wwweeelll, I take it you saw the 'thing' last night." Floyd flipped right side up again.

"What thing?"

"I think you would have remembered this 'thing' if you'd seen it," said Floyd, placing special emphasis on the word 'thing' every time it crossed his lips. "As concerned as Ramsay is about this 'thing', I would have thought his main man in Diterra would have paid at least a little attention to it."

"Floyd," said Noth, trying in vain to hide his irritation, "what 'thing' are you talking about?"

"Oh, nothing. Just the meteorite, the shooting star, the whatever-it-was that flew in from outer space last night and landed smack-dab in the middle of Diterra! That 'thing'! I take it you didn't see it, did you?"

"No," said Noth defensively, "I didn't."

"It's ok. You're only Ramsay's eyes and ears in this part of the garden. It's not like it matters to him or anything. Even though I've never seen him this worked up over anything, I'm sure he's fine with you not having any idea what's going on and needing me to fly all the way out here to tell you about it."

"Did you come all the way out here just to tell me that?"

"I certainly didn't fly all the way from the Hive, non-stop, just to see your gruesome face. But that's only part of Ramsay's message."

"Well? What's the rest of it?"

Floyd leaned his face nearer to Noth's and spoke slowly: "Get ... the 'thing'." As soon as he finished his sentence, Floyd stopped beating his wings and dropped out of Noth's line of sight. Then, somersaulting and corkscrewing in midair, he shouted, "Oh! You have no idea how good it feels to get that off my chest. Ramsay comes up to me and says, 'Floyd, I have an important job for you', and I'm all nervous. It's a lot of responsibility. It involves some travel. What if I screw it up? But I went, I did it—what a re-lief!"

Noth looked ill.

"Why so glum, Nothy-boy?" He didn't answer. Floyd stopped prancing to hover in front of Noth again. "Oh, I think I know. You have no idea how to find the 'thing', do you? I haven't given you enough information to go on, have I? You know you need something but you don't want to ask me—too proud to be helped by a lowly mosquito."

Noth had endured enough taunting. He shot spider silk out of his spinneret, caught it in his right forehand and snapped it like a whip around Floyd's mouth so he could not talk. In the next sec-ond, Noth spun even more silk and wrapped it around Floyd's body. Floyd, tied up and dangling upside-down, was not bothered in the least.

Noth lifted the silk rope until he could look Floyd in the face. "You wouldn't want to tell Ramsay the 'thing' got away be-cause you felt like screwing around, would you?"

"You make an excellent point," mumbled Floyd through the glob of silk covering his mouth. He wriggled an arm free, reached under his wing, and pulled out a small leaf with something written on it. "This shows where it landed."

Noth took the leaf from Floyd and cut him loose. He took a few moments to review the leaf, then dropped from his web and scurried toward the very spot where Waverly found Ben earlier that day.

***

With Ben laid safely on the cart, Waverly and Oliver each grabbed a handle and started pushing. Ms. Pourri kept a watchful eye on them.

"What are you doing?" Motioning to Ben, she added, "Who's that?"

"That's just our brother, Ben," answered Oliver without looking back at her.

"You didn't come here with a brother."

Waverly said, "That's right, we found him here."

"Well, more like we met him here," corrected Oliver.

"Yeah, but not like for the first time met him," said Waverly.

"Oh, yeah. He's our brother, so of course we've met him before," said Oliver. "Now we're taking him home ... to his home obviously."

"Looks like you're kidnapping him," the gruff, old bug stated bluntly.

"Oh, how silly," Waverly said. "Clearly, we're not kidnapping him."

"Well, we've got to go. See you next time." Oliver put his hand in the middle of Waverly's back and charged out of there. Walking on the road out of the city, it seemed every passing fly gave them a curious look. With each step, Waverly became increasingly aware of how suspicious they must appear. At the next possible opportunity, Waverly veered the cart off the main road into a darkened alley.

Dap and Ug stood with their backs against the wall—the same wall they had pinned Ben against less than an hour earlier. Noth prowled in front of them, looking very much like this was a matter of life and death. The dozens of spiders positioned behind him stood watch over their commander.

Noth questioned Dap and Ug at length. What had they seen? Where did that fly come from? Why wouldn't he speak? Who was the little girl? Did they prove they were related? Then what happened? The answer to this last question enraged Noth. "WHY DID YOU LET THEM GO?"

Ug looked to Dap, effectively casting blame on him. Suddenly, the reasons Dap had given Ug for letting them go seemed inadequate. He was unable to manage much more than unintelligible stammering in reply. Taking full advantage of Dap's helplessness, Ug said, "I argued against releasing them, but he pulled rank."

Dap's expression confirmed that Ug spoke the truth. Pointing a few arms at Dap, Noth bristled, "Ramsay himself wants this fly's carcass on a web and you let him go? As a reward for your mercy, I might send him yours instead. Arrest him!"

Noth's guards seized Dap even though he had been the leader of their squad. Dap forcefully resisted, for he knew what became of those taken to the Dung Heap, but he was soon subdued.

After Dap was hauled away, Noth ordered Ug and the remaining guards to put the city on lockdown and barricade all roads leading in and out of Diterra. Once the other spiders dispersed, Noth crept up to the fly-shaped hole in the ground, looked into it, and said, "What kind of fly could have done this?"

***

Waverly pushed the cart into the alley until it was hidden from the glow of the street light. Several drunken flies sat a few feet away, reveling in their own filth. They paid no attention to Waverly and Oliver.

"Are you crazy?" asked Oliver, whispering though he wanted to yell. "We've got to get out of here! Why are you stopping?"

"Everybody out there is staring at us, Oliver. Don't you realize how weird we look? If a spider sees us with a passed out fly on our cart, he would stop us for sure. We've got to hide Ben in the net under the cart."

Oliver hadn't thought of it this way before, but it made perfect sense considering it from the spiders' perspective. They lifted Ben off the cart and carefully stuffed him into the net. They doubted Ben was comfortable, but at least he was out of sight.

"Much better," said Oliver. "Now come on, let's get out of here."

"No, wait!"

Oliver, who had started pushing the cart, stopped suddenly and tipped his head back in exasperation at Waverly's delaying. "What now?"

"What if they're looking for us? What if they stopped us? Surely they would search our cart. They know our names, and you know they'll be looking for three flies—two boys and a girl. They'd never let us take him out of the city."

"But they let us go. Why would they be looking for us?"

"I don't know, but we have to be ready in case they are."

Before Oliver could reply, Waverly flew over to the alley flies. When she approached, they stood up and fell silent. They ex-

30

changed some words as Waverly pointed back at Oliver and the cart. The flies pointed toward the main street, and then swept their arms to the right, in the direction of the Beesleys' house. Waverly nodded and flew back to Oliver with three of the flies following close behind.

"Remember," she explained, "you get half now and half when we get the cart back. Oliver, I want you to head out of the city first. Wait for them somewhere you won't be seen. I won't be far behind." She handed some money and a raspberry Mr. Mosca had not taken to the three alley flies.

Oliver turned right out of the alley, onto the road leading out of the city. He was stunned to see the spiders hastily setting up a checkpoint under Diterra's welcome sign. No one could leave the city without being scrutinized by the spiders first. In all the years he had been coming to the market, he had never seen anything like this. His knees nearly buckled under the weight of knowing that they were looking for him.

He took a deep breath and stepped into the line as casually as he could. One of the spiders at the front of the checkpoint commanded: "Be thorough. Stop everyone. Remember you are looking for three flies—two boys and a girl."

Hearing the spider say it exactly as his sister had put it gave Oliver a renewed appreciation for her intelligence.

"And their names are Ben, Waverly, and Oliver."

Hearing the spider say their names nearly made him get sick. When he reached the front of the checkpoint, a spider grabbed Oliver by the wing and pulled him out of line. "Name?"

"O ..." He barely caught himself in time. "Oswald. My name is Oswald."

"Well, Oswald, why did you come all by yourself to Diterra today?"

"To meet a friend."

"Was your friend's name Oliver? Or was it Ben?" Oliver feared he was about to get squashed.

"N-no. His name's Guido."

"You came all the way to Diterra and you're not leaving with anything. How come?"

"My stuff got stolen."

"Who stole your stuff?"

"Guido."

The spider laughed in Oliver's face. "You flies are a joke. Get out of here, you're wasting my time."

Oliver left Diterra but felt no relief yet. He walked down the road a safe distance and pulled off to watch for the others.

A few minutes later, the three alley flies were at the front of the checkpoint with the cart. A different spider made a close examination of them and their cargo.

"What's this?" asked the spider, pulling back the net just enough to reveal Ben sleeping underneath. The garland of bluebells had wound around his neck.

"He's just had a little too much for his own good," said one of the alley flies, sounding like he was the one who had had too much. "We're making sure he gets home all right, all right, all right."

"Who is he to you?"

"Who is he to me? Who is he to me?" Oliver tensed up worrying whether the alley fly would give a passable answer to this question. After a long pause, Oliver was reduced to hoping the fly would give any answer at all. At last it came from a sentimental alley fly: "He's the reason I've got money to spend. He's the reason I've got food to eat." A little tear even trickled down his face. "Why, he's everything to me."

Before the spider could ask another question, his commander whispered in his ear, "We're looking for two boys and a girl. Enough with these drunks."

"Yes, sir," replied the spider. Turning back to the flies he said, "Get out of my sight. Go."

Oliver let out a sigh of relief when they rolled Ben through the checkpoint. Then he breathlessly waited for several eternal minutes until Waverly reached the front and was yanked out of line by the same spider who had questioned him.

"What's your name, maggot?"

"Daisy."

"Little too ugly for that name don't you think? If you're going to take a plant name, why not something more appropriate like Stinkweed or something?"

"I didn't pick it."

"Well, tell me, Stinkweed, what were you doing here today?"

"I sold some things."

"Were you with anybody?"

"Not really."

"Not really isn't the same as no, so who were you with?"

"Just my friend, Guido."

"Guido, huh? You sure you didn't hang around with a little guy named Oliver. Or was it Oswald?"

"No, it was only Guido. I don't know anybody named Oliver or Oswald." Her voice was steady despite the adrenaline racing through her body.

"Not sure I believe you." There was a painful silence between them as the spider stared down at Waverly. It took all her courage to stare right back at him.

Suddenly, a fight broke out two lines away and threatened to throw the whole checkpoint into chaos. The spider interrogating her jumped into the action to break up the fight and punish the flies involved. With him distracted, Waverly slipped past the checkpoint and out of the city.

Oliver ducked down and waited for Waverly. By the time she reached him, she had already paid off the alley flies and was pushing the cart on her own. He grabbed a handle, and they pushed the cart as fast as they could without looking like they were fleeing a crime scene. They were over half way home and nearly out of breath when they finally slowed down to a normal pace.

A flood of emotion surged within them. Relief swept in first. The elation that comes with narrowly escaping began as a trickle, but grew more powerful with every step. Fear was persistent as a riptide hidden under the surface, continually pulling at them, threatening to overtake them if given enough time. Of all their emotions, one rose above the others to be displayed on their faces: pride, the kind reserved for heroes.

As their home came into sight, Oliver broke the silence. "Waverly?"

"Yeah, Oliver?"

"Looks like your wish came true, huh?"

"I guess this counts as coming home with something special, but smuggling an unconscious fly out of the city wasn't exactly what I had in mind."

***

34

Noth sat high above Diterra on his web. The temperature had dropped drastically with nightfall, and the cold only worsened his already foul mood. Shivering and clinging to the side of a nearby building, Floyd was content to stay out of Noth's way.

One by one the spiders reported back, each bearing the same message: the checkpoints failed to discover the mysterious fly wanted by Ramsay. Each successive report of failure made Noth spit and yell and rage more violently than the last. His commanders shook with fear that they would find themselves the target of Noth's wrath.

With no leads, finding one fly in a city of thousands would be difficult. Only the most severe measures promised any hope of success. Noth assembled all the spiders under his command. "Nobody gets in or out of Diterra until we have gone door to door and searched every last room in this city for the fugitives. Your primary target is a fly named Ben. He was accompanied by two flies named Waverly and Oliver who claim to be his siblings. Obviously, they might have split up by now."

The commander responsible for the checkpoint that Oliver, the cart, and Waverly passed through shifted uneasily. The spider who interrogated them lowered his head, thankful he had not told anybody about the fly who got away.

Noth continued, "Make no mistake: if we do not find this Ben, Ramsay will have our heads. If you do find him, he cannot be harmed in any way. Ramsay wants to deal with him personally."

Then Noth doled out assignments to his commanders. "You two, take your troops to the neighboring cities and find reinforcements. We need every available spider. You four, your troops are to secure the perimeter—no one gets in or out. Everyone else, scour the city. Break down doors, knock buildings over if you have to, but every last inch of Diterra is to be searched until we find him. Now get to work!"

The spiders started to scatter, when Noth called out, "Not you, Ug. You're coming with me." Ug was left standing alone, tense and apprehensive.

"Relax," growled Noth. "You're going to help me rip Dap's arms off, that's all."

A ghoulish and relieved grin spread out across Ug's face. "Gladly."

***

Never had Waverly and Oliver been more comforted by the sight of their home. As they trudged up their hill, a strong wind blew and storm clouds gathered above. Pupa welcomed them home by lowering his head and chest to the ground while his butt wriggled in the air. Oliver greeted Pupa with a scratch behind the ears.

Waverly parked the cart, and together they pulled Ben out from his secret hideaway, carried him into their apple shelter, and laid him down. Pupa followed close behind, curiously sniffing Ben and anything he had touched. Ben lay motionless on the grass-covered floor, his chest barely rising as he breathed.

"Hard to believe," said Waverly yawning, "he could have slept through all that."

Other than a "good night," the flies were so utterly exhausted neither had anything left to say. Waverly washed her face and lay down. Oliver pulled a leaf over his body and Pupa curled up next to his feet. Within seconds, the clouds burst open and rain poured down. The gentle thwump-thwump-thwumpping sound of raindrops on their apple-skin roof made their home feel that much more like a safe haven. They slept that night blissfully unaware the hunt for them had just begun in earnest.

Chapter Five
Home

The cricket glided along the dark, empty corridor, his purple robe flowing behind him. The hood shielding his face hid white-as-cotton eyes and a sallow complexion. Every morning, minutes before sunrise, the cricket named Croda followed the same path to the same destination. Though he was blind, he never stumbled, never bumped into anything, never groped his way through the pitch black hallways. Croda simply glided. Some believed he counted his steps. Others said he was guided by his sense of smell. However he did it, the mystique surrounding him was only enhanced by the effortlessness with which he moved through total darkness.

After rounding a few corners and passing through a long corridor, Croda arrived at the throne room, where firelight dissected the darkness and two armed guards stood watch. The guards shuddered when they saw him for his power inspired genuine fear. Although Croda spent only a few minutes with Ramsay each day, his visits had a dramatic effect. With only a few words, he could conjure an insatiable, destructive jealousy in Ramsay, turn his good mood to rage, or restore him to relative calm. The guards stepped aside so he could pass by.

The throne room was enormous but sparsely decorated. A plain throne carved out of the front wall sat upon a platform directly opposite the entrance. Twisting staircases rose from the floor to the platform on either side of the throne. Dozens of worn out spider webs were scattered throughout the room, and a few torches hung from the walls. The slightest noise sent echoes bouncing around the chamber. High above the throne, Ramsay, the spider king with the glowing red eyes, rested on an impressive web. Inside the little white cocoons littering his web were the bugs who would soon become his morning meal.

The cricket glided up the staircase and knelt before his king. Ramsay dropped off the web, his eight feet clacking against the throne as he landed in it. "You may rise," said Ramsay, his deep voice filling the room. "Yesterday you told me a mighty rebellion would rise from Diterra."

"Yes, your majesty," replied Croda, his hoarse voice scarcely audible. "And I told you the rebel leader will arrive as suddenly as a comet and his light will burn out just as quickly."

"But you had no word for me regarding the outcome of this rebellion. My kingdom, indeed, my very life is at risk. I need to know this rebellion can be crushed. I need to know that I can make an example of the rebel leader for generations to come. Tell me, what word have you brought me today, my prophet?"

"Today's message hints at the path to victory, sire. The rebels may seem unimposing, but truly you have never confronted a greater threat. As you plan, however, know what I have seen: Victory belongs to him who fights closest to home."

"Closest to home, eh? Very well. But how to lure the rebels to the Hive?"

"This rebel leader has a weakness, a fatal flaw."

"Which is?"

"Loyalty," wheezed Croda. "He will not leave his friends to suffer alone. Further word than this I have not received."

"Very well, prophet. You have served me faithfully. You may take your leave."

Ramsay delighted in this revelation and devoted his thoughts to devising a strategy to save his kingdom. Croda descended the staircase and headed back to the dark recesses of the Hive where he spent his days in isolation. Before the train of the prophet's purple robe disappeared from the throne room, Ramsay had formulated his plan to destroy the rebel leader and quash the rebellion.

"Guards," he bellowed. They sprang dutifully into the throne room. "Inform the handlers of the Malicious Poison Spiders that they are to report to Diterra immediately. Here are their instructions," he said while scrawling on the back of a leaf with a silken spider thread. He handed over the leaf and barked, "Now get out. I'm hungry for breakfast." After they left, Ramsay climbed onto his web and bit into one of the little white cocoons.

***

The sun was up by the time Waverly started to kick her feet and turn from side to side. Its golden rays broke into their little house through an opening, shining brightly on her eyes but giving no warmth. She kicked and turned faster and faster until she woke, gasping and bolting upright. She looked for Oliver as she tried to catch her breath, but he was gone. Just then, she felt a hand on her arm and let loose a short, piercing scream.

"Are you okay?" asked Ben, who had been sitting on the floor next to her. The garland of bluebells still hung around his neck.

"I'm fine, I guess. Just had a really bad dream."

"What was it?"

"I was all by myself, stuck in the middle of a spider's web. That was bad enough, but then the web was pushed into a lake. I was sinking but couldn't do anything to save myself. It was terrible."

"Sounds terrible. I would never let that happen to you," said Ben. "Anyway, I'm glad you're awake. I was worried you might sleep all day."

"That's funny, I thought the same thing about you yesterday. How long have you been up?"

"A couple of hours."

"Where's Oliver?"

"He said he was getting us breakfast. Is he your husband?"

"Yuck, no! He's my brother. Besides, we're too young to be married."

At that moment, Oliver stomped into the house, his arms loaded with food. He had gathered chunks of pumpkin from a patch on the other side of their hill and some apples from their yard. Waverly and Oliver were excited to learn more about their guest over breakfast. Despite all their questions for him, he did not have many answers.

"I'm confused," he said. "You asked me my name, but you keep calling me Ben. Doesn't that mean my name is Ben?"

"That's just the name we gave you because we had to call you something," explained Waverly. "You must have had a name before we met you."

Ben stared at them blankly and shrugged his shoulders. "If I did, I can't think of it now. But I like Ben, so I'll stick with that."

"Is there anything you do remember before waking up here?" asked Oliver.

"I remember being at the bottom of a big hole."

"Don't you remember anything before that?" asked Oliver.

"Only that I was on my way home."

"Where were you coming from?"

"Beats me," said Ben, rather calmly for someone suffering a serious memory loss. "I woke up in that hole, and my head hurt. When I looked up, it was so bright and so loud, I couldn't think straight. But I remember climbing out and, come to think of it, I remember seeing you at the top," he said, pointing at Waverly.

"Anything else?" she asked.

He thought for a few seconds. "Nope. Just waking up here with you guys."

Waverly and Oliver looked at each other in disbelief. Yesterday was the most exciting and memorable day of their lives and Ben, the reason for it all, did not remember any of it.

"Well, Ben, my friend," said Oliver, "have we got a story for you!"

"How about we tell him outside?" said Waverly. "We need to get to work." It was still harvest season after all, and flies worked hard during the harvest. Even though they weren't sure when it would be safe to go back to the market, they behaved like life would return to normal soon. Little did they know their lives would never be anything that could be considered normal again.

When the flies started work in their yard, the spiders had already been busy at work back in the city. The reinforcements they summoned trickled into Diterra at a steady pace and the spiders had constructed enormous webs over the city to prevent any flies from escaping. Throughout Diterra, the spiders kicked down doors, barged into homes, knocked holes into walls, broke anything they touched, and roughed up every fly they saw.

No one in Diterra ever labored under the illusion that spiders cared in the slightest for the flies, but never had they acted with such disregard for them. From every corner of the city where the spiders had finished unleashing their fury, the flies were heard to whisper:

"Who is this Ben they're after?"

"I heard Ramsay himself is after him."

"I was sitting at home minding my own business, then they broke in and destroyed everything ..."

"If I found Ben, I'd turn him in."

"I'd punch him in the gut, then turn him in."

"An enemy of Ramsay would be a friend of mine."

"... absolutely everything. I've got nothing left. Nothing!"

"Wonder what he did?"

"It must have been something big. He's got Ramsay spooked."

The flies of Diterra had an awful night and their day was only going to get worse.

***

Out in their yard, the flies sorted through fallen apples as Waverly and Oliver excitedly recounted for Ben everything that happened in Diterra the day before. He was amazed to learn all they had done for him and all he had slept through.

After finishing their story and their work, Ben asked, "Isn't it weird that I can't remember anything?"

"It's definitely unusual," said Waverly. "You must have hit your head pretty hard."

"But you didn't forget everything. You remembered you were on your way home," Oliver reminded him.

"That's true," said Ben.

"Maybe going home would jog your memory, remind you of all the things you forgot," said Oliver.

"But I can't remember where it is."

"We could help you find it," offered Waverly. "Do you have any idea about which part of Diterra you live in?"

"I don't think I lived in Diterra."

"If you don't live in the city," Waverly said, "you definitely live near it. Who knows, maybe you live close to us?"

"That doesn't sound right either. I feel like I was just passing through, like I'm not from around here at all."

"Believe me," said Oliver, "you're a fly, and all flies are from Diterra. It's one of Ramsay's rules: all insects must keep to their own. That means all the flies have to live together in our designated area."

"What are Ramsay's rules?" asked Ben.

"Ramsay rules this garden," Waverly replied. "The other spiders and bugs have to do what he says. His rules are the law. Break Ramsay's rules and you're in big trouble."

"What kind of big trouble?"

"The Dung Heap," stated Oliver. "When a spider finds out a bug has broken a rule—POOF—the bug disappears, and no one ever hears from him again. But everybody knows he's been taken to the Dung Heap. We think that's what happened to our Mom and Dad."

"That's a cruel way to run things!" said Ben. "Why would Ramsay do that?"

"Ramsay says it's the only just way to run things," answered Waverly. "He says it's unfair to get something you don't deserve, and if you break a rule, then you deserve punishment."

"This might sound dumb, but why not just follow Ramsay's rules?" asked Ben.

"It can't be done," said Oliver. "He has so many rules it's impossible to follow them all. Some rules even contradict other rules, so there's no way you could obey them both at the same time."

"That hardly seems fair," said Ben.

"That's the point. It's so we don't have a chance," Oliver replied.

"In fact," said Waverly, "the spiders say that bugs break the rules because we were born rule-breakers, and that's all we'll ever be."

"But bugs are born for so much more than that. And to do so much more than just ending up on some stupid Dung Heap," said Ben.

"That's exactly what Mom and Dad used to tell us too," Waverly stated. Then no one said anything. Sadness crept in and hung in the air between them.

After a while, Ben addressed the sadness at its source: "Is there anyone else in your family now or is it just the two of you?"

"It's just us," said Waverly, discreetly wiping her eye. "But another thing our parents told us was that family is the people you love, whether they're related to you or not."

"If that's the case, you've made me feel like I'm part of your family already."

"That's good," Oliver said, "because until you can remember your name, when you're with us, you're not just Ben, you're Ben Beesley."

CHAPTER SIX
FIXING A HOLE

Though the spiders spent hours laying Diterra to ruin, it brought them no closer to finding what they were looking for. Noth was so concerned about what Ramsay might do to him if he did not find Ben, he scarcely enjoyed terrorizing the flies or destroying their city. He was watching the bedlam he had unleashed, growing more despondent by the minute, when two spiders arrived at his web. "We think we have something you'd be interested in, sir," they said.

Noth followed them to a ramshackle building with a gaping hole in its side. There, pinned under a wooden plank fallen from the ceiling, lay Ms. Pourri, the gruff fly from the market. "I know something about the bugs you're looking for, but I'm only talking if you promise to get me out of here."

"I assure you, we will give you the all help you deserve for your cooperation," Noth said. "However, I'm sure you'll understand if I insist on the information first."

"Waverly and Oliver Beesley—I saw them leaving the city yesterday with a strange fly they claimed was their brother, but I know they don't have any brother. It looked very suspicious."

"Did you catch the name of their brother?" asked Noth.

"Ben," answered Ms. Pourri. "And they left on that road," pointing to the street that led out of Diterra and right past the Beesleys' house.

"Is there anything else?"

"I reckon that's it. Can you help me out of here now, like you promised?"

"Old woman," said Noth harshly, "I promised to give you only what you deserved. Under Ramsay's rules you're required to give assistance willingly in official investigations. You, however, kept silent until you needed help, then tried to extort your way out of trouble. What you deserve is to be left here. We'll come back for you in a week. If you're still alive, we'll send you to the Dung Heap."

Noth raced off to put this new intelligence to good use. Turning back to the spiders he shouted, "And rebuild that wall so no one has to put up with her crying."

***

Having chased their sadness away by cracking a couple of jokes, Oliver scooped up some mud left behind by the rain and rolled it into a ball. They passed the mud ball back and forth until Oliver threw it too hard and too high. It sailed over Ben's head, landed in Mrs. Galway's yard, and rolled up next to her house.

Mrs. Galway was mean when Waverly and Oliver walked on the path by her house; she turned downright wicked if they stepped foot in her yard. Before they could warn Ben of the dan-

48

ger, he had raced onto her property to fetch their ball. "Ben!" Oliver shouted. "Just let it go. I'll make another one."

As he approached Mrs. Galway's house, Ben heard a loud crash come from within. A moment of quiet followed before Mrs. Galway hollered, "If you're in my yard, my house better be on fire, and you better be carrying a hose." Ben bent down to pick up their ball. "I'll make you wish you were never born if you take one more step." Mrs. Galway sounded so strangely close to him, he expected to see her rounding the corner of the house and trying to beat him over the head with her cane.

Rather than run, Ben waited. Waverly and Oliver stood at the edge of her lawn begging him to run away as fast as he could. But Ben was too intent on listening to Mrs. Galway to hear them. The more she yelled, the more it sounded like she was in the backyard, yet she never came around front to chase him away. She just kept yelling.

Instead of flying to safety, Ben walked around to the rear of her house. To his surprise, he did not see Mrs. Galway at the back door or standing in her yard. Instead, he saw there was no back door at all—only a giant hole in her wall. The large branch that had fallen on her home was still there. Ben could tell it had been like this for months.

He looked through the hole and at last laid eyes on Mrs. Galway. She was on the floor, sprawled out on her back, with her feet tangled in a twig she had tripped over. Her cane was stuck in the wall, and she jerked her arm in a vain attempt to shake it loose. A white film blanketed her eyes, and she spewed a flurry of threats—threats now revealed to have been empty all along. Seeing this blind, old fly so scared and so vulnerable filled Ben with compassion for her.

Waverly and Oliver were aghast when Ben disappeared behind Mrs. Galway's house.

"What's he doing?" Oliver asked.

"Trying to get himself killed, obviously."

Indeed, years of enduring Mrs. Galway's threats had made Waverly and Oliver certain that meeting her face to face would be a veritable suicide mission. They hadn't saved Ben from spiders only to watch him get devoured by their cranky neighbor. They ran around to the back of the house. Seeing the enormous hole surprised them, but it was the sight of Ben trying to talk to Mrs. Galway that was truly startling.

"You take one step closer and I'll thump you good." She tugged on her cane with a renewed sense of urgency.

"Mrs. Galway," Ben said while sinking to his knees, "let me help you get up."

"How do you know my name? Get out of here! Just take what you want and leave me alone!"

"What I want is for you to let me help you," said Ben. "Please?"

After hearing the word, "please," Mrs. Galway changed. Whatever it was inside of her that was always ready to fight gave in to Ben. In that moment, she was no longer angry or afraid, but trusting. "Yes," she whispered and held out her hand.

Waverly and Oliver stared in disbelief. They had lived next to Mrs. Galway their entire lives and had never heard her utter a single word without yelling.

Ben rolled the twig away from her feet, took Mrs. Galway's hands, and helped her up. He led her to a chair and helped her sit. Waverly and Oliver, trying to suppress their shock, came closer and introduced themselves. She said hello back.

50

As they talked, Mrs. Galway told them about her life and how she came to live on their hill. She told them about her husband and kids, and how one day, they went to the market and never came home. Mrs. Galway turned to friends and neighbors for help, but no one came to her aid. Instead, they kept their distance. Worse, the other bugs began to mock her sorrow, once even tricking her into believing her husband had returned when he had not. Her tormentors realized no one ever came to her defense, and they started stealing from her. Eventually they moved into her house and forced her to leave. To escape, she resettled as far away from Diterra as she was allowed to go.

Her hope of being left alone was dashed when two families moved onto her hill with the apple tree. But by that time, she had masterfully honed her defenses. All the meanness she heaped on Waverly, Oliver, and anyone else who got near her had the effect she intended: it kept everyone away. Despite her resourcefulness—she built her home with her own hands after all—her blindness and the frailty that came with old age left her unable to fix her house. It was only when Ben found her, helpless in her own home, that she knew she needed someone.

For the first time in their lives, Waverly and Oliver began to understand Mrs. Galway. To their surprise, they actually liked her and wanted to help her as best they could. Ben fetched her some apples to eat. Waverly cleaned the mess Mrs. Galway had let build up over the years, and Oliver even made her laugh a little.

Having addressed the problems inside, the Beesleys addressed the hole in Mrs. Galway's wall. With a sharp piece of flint rock, Ben chopped the branch into pieces, which Waverly and Oliver disposed of. Next, they built a frame to fit over the hole by tying twigs together with blades of grass. At Waverly's suggestion, they glued a large patch of apple skin over the frame using tree sap, then glued the frame to the house. As a finishing touch, they painted the new addition with the indigo they brought home from the market. Mrs. Galway's place looked like a house again.

Mrs. Galway beamed when she surveyed their work and declared her house was warmer already. But she soon added she was getting sleepy, and the Beesleys took that as a signal that it was time to go. On their way out the door, Mrs. Galway thanked them all and said, "Something about you, Ben, reminds me of them, but they haven't been in this garden for a long, long time."

"Who's that?" asked Ben.

"The bees. Something about you reminds me of the bees."

"Aah, thank you," Ben said hesitantly. Then he took off the garland of bluebells and placed it around her neck. "This is for you."

Mrs. Galway inhaled deeply. "Bluebells. Such a lovely fragrance."

After saying their goodbyes, the Beesleys closed her door. On the walk back to their yard, Ben asked, "What did she mean about the bee thing?"

"Don't you know about the bees?" asked Waverly in surprise.

Ben shook his head.

"How could you not know the story of the bees and the spiders? Waverly, we have to tell him," Oliver said.

"Ok," Waverly answered, "but we better do it inside."

***

The spiders unleashed the same havoc along the road out of Diterra as they had in the city itself. Noth and Floyd were inspect-

52

ing the damage when two groups of spiders charged at them from opposite directions. The smaller group, coming from the direction of the Beesleys' house, got to them first.

"Sir! Sir!" they called, nearly out of breath. "We've found them! Witnesses put them at a house on a hill about fifteen minutes from here."

"Well done," said Noth. "Let's get them."

"But sir!" shouted a member of the group coming the other way. There were six spiders altogether, two of which were being pushed in barred cages on wheels. "You should read this first."

Irritated to be kept from catching his prey, Noth ripped the message from the spider's hand. It was from Ramsay. After a quick read, Noth looked up and said, "Change of plans. We're not going after them; they need to come to us. Floyd, fly ahead to figure out how we can bait a trap."

CHAPTER SEVEN
THE RACE

Waverly, Oliver, and Ben were headed into their house when they heard Pupa yelping. He was far off but coming closer by the second.

"I wonder what he's upset about," Waverly said.

"Puu-paa," Oliver called, "come here boy."

As Pupa charged up the hill toward them, sludgy, brown gunk dripped off his body, leaving a trail of filth behind him.

"Wow! He really stinks," said Ben, even though Pupa was still ten feet away.

Pupa ran straight to Oliver with a playful look in his eyes. Despite Oliver's pleading, Pupa jumped into the air and smacked into Oliver, smearing the mucky goop all over him. Oliver forced Pupa to the ground and held him there until he settled down. The stench nearly knocked the flies over.

"What happened to you, boy?" Oliver asked.

"Hey Beesley," said a voice from down the hill. "Hope you don't mind, but we gave Poop a bath."

"He looked way too clean," said a second all-too-familiar voice.

It was the Lockwood boys. Although neighbors since birth, the years had intervened to make the Beesleys and the Lockwoods both strangers and rivals. Waverly, as the oldest child and only girl, generally stayed above the fray. She found Todd and Chip Lockwood's strange competitiveness childish. Oliver, however, lacked her perspective. His easy-going nature belied a hot temper and a pride that would not allow him to turn a blind eye to their juvenile antics. Unfortunately, both Todd and Chip were at least a head taller than Oliver. With Waverly a conscientious objector to their skirmishes, he usually got the worse of his match-ups against not one, but two oversized opponents.

Abusing his beloved pet by coating him in sludgy mud—how Oliver hoped it was only sludgy mud—usually would have resulted in a war of words that escalated into real fighting that left Oliver on the losing end. But this day was different; Ben was there.

"Why did you do this to him?" shouted Oliver. "He can't defend himself!"

"He was in our yard," said Chip. "We warned you that if your mutt-maggot didn't keep out of our yard, we'd have to do something about it." The Lockwoods crowded so close to Oliver that his protruding belly bumped against them and he had to crane his head up just to maintain eye contact.

"He wasn't hurting you!"

"Well, what are you going to do about it?" Chip asked.

The moment before their argument would have escalated into a real fight, Ben said, "I think you should clean him up."

He startled Chip and Todd. They had been exclusively focused on antagonizing Oliver and had not noticed Ben, who stood just enough taller than both boys to make them relax their threatening stances a bit.

"Who are you?" Chip demanded.

"I'm Ben."

"He's staying with us for a while," said Waverly. "He's a family friend."

"Your family doesn't have any friends, and you know it," taunted Chip.

"You were probably at Ol' Lady Galway's place begging her to be your friend so you can say you have at least one," said Todd.

"I am their friend," said Ben. "And I think you two should clean up Pupa."

"You going to make us?" asked Chip.

"I guess I can't make you," said Ben, "but I'm willing to bet you."

"Bet us?"

"Yep. If you two can beat me and Oliver in a race, we'll clean him up. But if we win, then you do it."

"Or we don't bet anything, and you guys clean him up," Chip said.

"That's fine," Ben replied. "I'd be worried about losing too, if I were you."

"Losing? Are you kidding?" said Chip. Pointing at Oliver he added, "He's the slowest runner in Diterra, probably the whole garden. We'd kill you."

"Not a foot race," said Ben.

"You've seen his stubby wings, right? There's no way you'd beat us flying."

"I don't mean flying either. We're challenging you to a leaf race."

"What's a leaf race?"

"It's easy. Both teams take a leaf to the top of this hill and, after a running start, ride down on it together. First team to the bottom wins, and the losers give Pupa a real bath."

"You're on," said Chip.

Each team searched for a suitable racing leaf. The Lockwoods settled on a wide, red maple, while Ben and Oliver chose a skinny, yellow elm. As the teams trudged up the hill with their leaves, Oliver nervously said, "Ben, I've got to tell you something."

"What is it?"

"Thanks for helping me out back there and everything—I don't want you to think I don't appreciate it—but I've never won a race in my life. In case you haven't noticed, I'm not really built for speed."

"I think you're made for this kind of race, Oliver, you just don't know it yet. With leaf racing, the heavier you are the faster you go. Plus, the type of leaf you use makes a big difference. Believe me, ours will be much faster than theirs." Discovering how clever his new friend was put a smile on Oliver's face.

Once they reached the top, the racers took their places and looked down the hill. Ben asked the Lockwoods if they wanted to practice first. "We don't need practice to beat you two," Chip snapped.

Waverly stepped between the two teams and faced them. "All right—on my signal."

Ben positioned the elm leaf sled between himself and Oliver with the stem pointed down the hill. "Oliver," Ben said, "you'll steer, so take hold of this stem."

Oliver did as he was told and focused his eyes on Waverly. If only he could run as fast as his heart was beating, he would win for sure.

Waverly said, "Ready …"

Todd and Chip repositioned their leaf while they talked over which of them would do what and when. Though neither of the Lockwoods had ever heard of leaf racing before, one would have thought Chip had years of experience the way he barked orders at Todd.

"Steady …"

Both teams imagined their path to victory down that long, steep hill—past their houses, over the dusty road to Diterra, through a meadow, up a dirt mound, all the way to the half-empty pond that marked the finish line—and braced themselves for Waverly's signal.

"Go!"

Both teams tightly gripped their leaves and charged down the hill. Oliver ran as fast as he could but started to fall behind after a few quick steps.

"Oliver," Ben shouted, "hop on!"

Oliver jumped into the air, the stem clutched in his fists. While Oliver was airborne, Ben drove their leafy sled further downhill with a sudden burst of speed. Oliver landed belly first, sprawled out on the elm leaf, nearly twenty feet beyond where he first left the ground. A second after Oliver was securely on board, Ben plopped down behind him—a successful push-off completed.

Chip and Todd ran down the hill in perfect unison with their maple leaf sled between them. They were quick; much faster than Ben and Oliver. As if they had been practicing the move for weeks, the Lockwoods took simultaneous flying leaps as they tucked their leaf underneath themselves. It was the perfect start and the lead was theirs to lose.

Both teams zipped down the hill, leaving Waverly and Pupa to watch from the top. The strength of the wind whipping against their faces surprised them and dried out their eyes. Neither team had appreciated how bumpy the hill would seem when hurling down it with such great speed, and both struggled to stay on their leaves.

Ben and Oliver were gaining on Team Lockwood when a rotten apple fell from the tree, plunking down directly in front of them. Oliver yanked the steering-stem hard to the left. They narrowly missed the apple, but veering so abruptly had thrown Ben off the leaf. He caught hold of Oliver's wing—poor Oliver felt like it might get ripped right off his back—which allowed him to regain his balance enough to climb back on.

"Good driving," said Ben. "Don't worry, we'll still catch them." They had fallen further behind, but at least they hadn't smashed into rotten fruit, a small consolation if they lost to Chip and Todd.

Todd looked over his shoulder. "We're beating them."

"Watch what you're doing!" shouted Chip.

The Lockwoods skidded across the road to Diterra a few seconds ahead of Ben and Oliver. In the meadow it became apparent the Beesleys' choice of leaf was much better than the Lockwoods'. The slender elm allowed them to keep picking up speed once the wide maple reached its maximum velocity.

When Oliver and Ben sped into the lead, Chip screamed at Todd, "You're doing it wrong."

Todd yelled back, "It's not me, it's our leaf. It's too wide."

"Well do something!"

"We have to make it smaller." With that, each brother started ripping off the sides of their leaf even as they barreled ahead at full speed.

At the bottom of the hill, Oliver and Ben shot up the large earthen ramp that had looked like only a small incline from the top. They launched into the air like a cannonball, shooting across the sky until the pond—a generous description of the large half-filled mud puddle—was directly beneath them. Clutching their leaf like a life raft, Ben and Oliver skipped four times across the water before plowing through it. When they came to a stop they were still dry, and they knew they had won.

Chip and Todd were so preoccupied with trimming their sled they did not notice the ramp until they hit it. They shot into the air and immediately lost control of their leaf and tumbled off the back. Without their weight on it, the leaf gently floated to the ground. Gravity was not as kind to Chip and Todd. They twisted and turned a few somersaults, never able to stabilize themselves long enough to give their wings a chance to work. Instead of winning the race, instead of even a graceful second place finish, they landed head first in the puddle.

Ben and Oliver rushed over to check on them. Todd crawled out, covered from top to toes by the foul-smelling sludge. Chip was so stuck that Ben and Oliver had to grab onto his legs to pull him loose. "Are you okay?" Oliver asked.

"I'm not okay! " shouted Chip. "You cheated!"

"What do you mean?" asked Ben.

"You set us up," said Chip. "You knew that would happen."

"Are you serious?" asked Ben. "We didn't mean for this to happen, it just ... happened."

"Get lost. And you can forget about us washing your stupid pet."

How Oliver wanted to force them to honor their wager, but he was not about to yield a bit of the satisfaction he felt by getting agitated. No matter what he said, Chip and Todd would not lay a finger on Pupa now that they were supposed to. "If you won't, I can't make you. I hate to run guys, but all this winning made me tired, and I've got to clean Pupa before bed."

Ben and Oliver started the walk home, leaving the Lockwoods covered in slop at the edge of the pond. Waverly jumped up and down celebrating their win as she ran down the hill. Pupa, following right on her heels, suddenly did not look quite so dirty, at least compared to Chip and Todd.

When they were far enough away for a private conversation, Oliver turned to Ben and exclaimed, "That ... was ... awesome! I've never beaten them at anything! Did you see their faces? And leaf racing? Where did you come up with that? That was genius!"

"Get used to it," said Ben. "You and I are going to take on this whole garden and win—I can feel it."

Waverly met them both with big hugs. Putting their arms around each other, they marched up the hill to their home, victorious.

***

Chip and Todd were trudging back home, talking over ways of getting revenge, when Floyd came flying by. He took one look at them covered with mud and said, "That's a great look, but you're going to need more mud over your face 'cause I can still tell you're ugly."

"Why don't you get lost, you dumb skeeter," yelled Chip.

"Seriously, you are so ugly your mom would need to tie a rancid pork chop around your neck just to get a maggot to play with you."

"Go suck someone else's blood, you six-legged vampire," said Todd, having had enough humiliation for one evening.

Floyd, remembering he had work to do, shut his mouth and kept flying. He was nearly out of ear shot when the Lockwood boys quit complaining about him long enough to say, "We should sic that nasty mosquito on Ben and Oliver. That would teach them."

Floyd whipped back toward Chip and Todd. "Boys, boys," he said. "Please accept my sincerest and most humble apologies. I honestly thought you were somebody else. I've got bad eyesight, and it wasn't until I heard you speak ... well anyway, I'm very sorry. Please forgive me."

Without giving them any time to respond, he said, "Did you say Ben and Oliver? They weren't the ones who covered you in mud, were they?"

Detecting some sympathy, they both nodded.

"That's just terrible," said Floyd with feigned sincerity. "And I feel so bad having added insult to your injury. Let me make it up to you. Would you like some help getting back at them?"

CHAPTER EIGHT
HISTORY LESSON

The sun set, and the flies settled down for the night. Having finally had his long-awaited bath, Pupa was allowed in the house again. After a nice dinner of raspberry and apple, the Beesleys rested comfortably on their floor. Oliver reminded Waverly of her promise to tell the story about the spiders and the bees. True to her word, she told the tale of how Ramsay came to rule the garden:

"There once was a time when this garden didn't exist. The land we're sitting on was a boring, empty field that stretched mile after mile in every direction. Until one day a Queen Bee came along who thought, *Surely this desolate spot is the perfect place to make the most beautiful garden in the world.* Many said she was crazy, but she could see what they could not.

"Her first job was to fill it with the most wonderful flowers she could find. She flew all around the world time and time again searching for just the right plants. When she discovered an exceptionally beautiful flower, she'd carry it all the way back to her garden no matter how far away it was. After years of hard work, the Queen assembled the most amazing collection of plants in the whole world. And they grew side by side, right in her garden.

"Having brought these plants from thousands of miles away, next she had to make sure each one had what it needed to thrive. She studied her flowers, learning exactly what each required in terms of water, sunlight, shade, food, and friendship. Knowing their thirst, she forged a river that ran over- and underground through the garden to deliver the perfect amount of water to every single plant. The Queen filled the soil with nutrients to make her plants healthy and strong. She planted trees to give shade and even landscaped the earth, adding a mountain here and a valley there until it was perfect.

"When she finished, she accomplished exactly what she had set out to do: hers was the most brilliant garden the world had ever seen. Everyone marveled at what she had done. They said, 'Anybody who could create something so wonderful must be wonderful herself.' Indeed she was, and everyone wanted to be near the Queen.

"She could have kept it all for herself, but the Queen was no fool. She knew something so beautiful must be shared so she invited the bees from her colony to join her. They were eager to be with her and happily accepted.

"But she wasn't done yet. She set out on another search, this time for the world's most incredible bugs. Soon she brought to her garden every kind of insect imaginable: flies, ants, termites, fireflies, butterflies, ladybugs, moths, dragon flies, fleas, beetles, crickets, grasshoppers, and on and on. And, in what would prove to be a fateful decision, she even brought spiders, which were six-legged insects at the time. The Queen loved her bugs, and they loved her back. Together, they worked to keep the garden beautiful.

"She gave the bees special positions, calling them guardians of the realm. From the other bugs, she chose one of each kind to be on a sort of governing council. Those bugs supervised the work of the garden and ensured that not even the tiniest detail was neglected. In addition to caring for her plants, the council made sure every one of her insects had all their needs met. If any bug encountered a problem, her hand-picked representatives had the authority to help.

"One of the Queen's favorite bugs was a smart and powerful spider named Ramsay. He had distinguished himself by his service to the Queen and was almost as good and wise as she was. As time passed, the Queen gave him greater and greater responsibility. And Ramsay loved his Queen. At least it seemed like he did.

"Winning such great favor with the Queen caused unforeseen problems. Ramsay came to see himself as superior to the other bugs; he saw the Queen alone as his equal. One fateful day, a bug in his charge asked for an audience with the Queen. His pride had grown so great he took this simple request as an insult and an attempt to undermine him. He worried the bug was trying to take his place of favor with the Queen. Ramsay burned with anger and treated the bug with great cruelty.

"The Queen realized Ramsay's pride had grown dangerous and that envy threatened to consume him. Out of grave concern, she reminded him that without humility it would be impossible for him to love and serve the bugs in her garden. She also reminded him of her incredible love for him.

"*Why*, wondered Ramsay, *would she tell me these things?* His suspicion had been so aroused, he couldn't accept that she honestly meant what she said.

"Some time later, the Queen declared she would take a journey beyond the garden. She appointed Gron, a leader among the bees, to rule in her absence. Gron was loyal and fair and had served the Queen since the beginning. She knew Ramsay expected to be put in charge, but she hoped that serving Gron would gently remind him the need for humility. Before she departed, the Queen pulled Ramsay aside and told him, 'I want you to serve Gron as you would me. I love you, and I'm counting on you.'

"Shortly afterwards, she said goodbye. It would be the last time anyone saw the Queen in the garden.

"Ramsay was livid. *How could the Queen do this to me if she truly loved me? I am the first among the most noble of all the species, yet she expects me to play slave to some second-rate bee. Does she think spiders are inferior to bees?* Anger consumed him. Soon he could think of nothing other than making the Queen pay for her insult.

"Some time after the Queen left, Gron came to Ramsay with a request. Nobody knows for certain what Gron asked of him. Some say he asked for advice. Others say he wanted Ramsay to lead an expedition to save some bugs trapped in the mountains. Whatever Gron's request, it set Ramsay off.

"Rather than serve Gron as the Queen had asked, Ramsay killed him with his own hands. He felt no shame for he was certain Gron got what he deserved for breaking the first of what would become Ramsay's rules: there is no one greater than Ramsay.

"But Ramsay grew fearful wondering what the Queen would do to him when she came back. While he felt the Queen deserved the blame for putting him in such a situation, he knew she would punish him. Not wanting to find himself at the Queen's mercy, Ramsay decided he could not allow her to return to the garden—she would come back only over his dead body.

"Ramsay knew he couldn't keep the Queen out of the garden himself; he would have to turn others against her. So before word of Gron's murder spread, Ramsay called all the spiders to the Hive. He told them the Queen no longer loved them and was plotting against them.

"They didn't believe him ... at first. But Ramsay was as persuasive as he was insistent. He asked if they noticed how spiders always got the worst jobs compared to the other bugs, and whether the Queen thought they wouldn't notice how she treats them worse than slaves or how she favors bees over all other bugs. Slowly, he convinced them that maybe the Queen was not so fair after all.

"Once he moved them to question the Queen's goodness, Ramsay knew he had them. He continued to push: 'It is my unfortunate duty to inform you that the bees are planning to attack us. And isn't it convenient for the Queen to leave the garden now so she can deny having known about this attack in case it backfires?'

"'How can you know this?' questioned a spider.

"Having led them to this question, Ramsay had his answer ready: 'I know because she had Gron try to kill me first. Regrettably, I was forced to take his life in self-defense. Having never encountered brutality before, I know you will find such a senseless tragedy difficult to accept. That is why—though it grieves my spirit to share it with you—I brought proof.' Once Ramsay presented Gron's lifeless body to them, the spiders believed every last word.

"'What can we do to save ourselves?' the spiders asked.

"Ramsay answered in a puffed up voice, like he thought it was his first speech as king. 'The Queen taught us that we were all equals even as she raised her bees up to rule over us. She told us that we have no enemies even as she mobilized an army against us. If you doubt me, then ask yourself: Is the Queen a spider or a bee? If the Queen's bees come after the spiders, who will come to our defense? The gnats? Mosquitoes? No! And what good would it do if they did. I'm afraid we are our only hope. We must rise up and kill the bees before they kill us.'

"The spiders let out a great cheer. The time for questioning was over. It was time for war, but they did not declare their war. Instead, they scattered throughout the garden, invited bees into their homes, and ambushed them. The poor bees didn't know what hit them.

"The bees who had not been tricked were terrified. They had never known violence and didn't know what to do now that they were the targets of it. But a young bee rose up to lead them. He believed peace and harmony could be restored. He urged the bees not to retaliate, saying, 'Surely, this is a grave misunderstanding. If only we can talk to the spiders, then we can restore the peace.' He pleaded with all the bugs in the garden, urging them to love and serve one another as the Queen would want them to. He told them that warring against each other would break her heart, and she deserved much better than that.

"Ramsay took advantage of the bees' good intentions. He told the new leader he was deeply saddened by all that had happened and would do everything in his power to stop the fighting. He proposed that all the bees and all the spiders meet at the Hive for a celebration of peace.

"Tragically, the bees believed Ramsay to be a bug of peace and accepted his invitation. The day of the gathering, every single bee traveled to the Hive and the spiders welcomed them with open arms. But while the bees expected a restoration of friendship, the spiders had prepared for a final showdown. After the last bee entered, the Hive was sealed up and the slaughter began. Only one bee managed to escape, but he fled the garden, and no one has seen a bee here since.

"On that day the spiders went into the Hive as insects with six legs. But after the slaughter, they came out with eight legs and preyed on insects from that day forward.

"The other bugs were appalled to learn of the spiders' deceit and viciousness. In solidarity with the bees, some bugs started wearing yellow and black coats. They tried to fill the void left by the bees' disappearance by caring for the garden and protecting the other bugs as the bees used to. They led a resistance against the spiders, hoping they could last long enough for the Queen to return and set things right.

"This only made Ramsay madder. He crowned himself King and outlawed the Queen. The spiders gathered to watch his coronation and shouted, 'The Queen is dead. Long live King Ramsay.' But a strange thing happened when the crown was placed on Ramsay's head. Rather than looking regal, he screamed in pain because it burned him. He quickly flipped it off his head, but it hit him in the middle of his back on its way to the ground. The crown singed his fur, leaving brown burn marks on his back and a ring around the top of his head. Never again did he try to wear the crown.

"In his first act as King, he declared it unlawful for any bug to wear the coat of a bee. Violators were sent to the Dung Heap. Hundreds of new rules followed, each carrying the same punishment if broken. The Queen's rules had encouraged the bugs to love and serve one another; Ramsay's made them fearful, selfish, and mistrusting.

"Gradually, the bugs who wore the bee coats disappeared. They were either sent to the Dung Heap or gave up their coats because they were so scared. Nevertheless, a few bugs bravely kept serving the Queen even though it was too dangerous to wear their coats publicly. To them, the Queen, not Ramsay, was the rightful ruler of the garden, and they kept following her. When one of her loyalists saw someone break one of Ramsay's rules to be kind to another bug, they would say, 'You wear her coat well.'

"But loyalty to the Queen came at a cost, for Ramsay's anger knew no bounds against those who refused to acknowledge his kingship. He had them arrested and taken to the Dung Heap, where they were forced into back-breaking, bone-crushing labor. After a long time on the Dung Heap, Ramsay gave them a chance to swear an oath of loyalty to him. Whether they swore an oath or they refused, Ramsay had them killed. The bugs were wrapped from head to toe in spider silk and then eaten.

"Year after year passed, and the Queen still didn't return. With each passing day, Ramsay got more ruthless, and more and more bugs began to doubt she was ever coming back. Doing good deeds and showing kindness soon became so dangerous that no one dared for fear they would end up on the Dung Heap. The only thing that mattered was staying alive, and the only way to do that was by following Ramsay's rules.

"With bugs no longer working together, the garden started to wither. Beautiful plants were choked by thorny weeds. Water, which had always been abundant, was hoarded. Flowers dried up, and round, ripe fruit shriveled, leaving nearly inedible things growing in their place. Vibrant colors faded and turned dingy and gray.

Eventually, a thick haze, which the sun could barely peak through, settled permanently in the sky, making it seem as though nature itself had given up on the garden.

"That's why the garden looks the way it does, that's what happened to the bees, and that's how Ramsay came to be King," Waverly said, ending her tale with a dramatic flourish.

After a moment, Oliver asked, "What do you think happened to the Queen?"

"Some say Ramsay had her killed. Others say she heard about what happened and was afraid to come back. But I think she was so heartbroken, she couldn't come back."

"Do you think she's forgotten about us?" asked Oliver.

"She couldn't if she tried," said Ben. "In fact, she's working right now to save us from Ramsay."

"Do you really think so?" asked Oliver, marveling at the possibility. Ben nodded. "But I thought you didn't know anything about the bees?"

"It all came back to me as I was listening."

"Maybe that means you're getting your memory back. That will make it a lot easier for us to find your home," said Waverly.

"Getting me home will be anything but easy," said Ben. "It's late. We need to get some sleep."

Although the darkness enveloped them and their weary bodies craved rest, they could not stop talking. They talked about what it would be like if the bees came back to free them from the spiders. They talked about standing up to Ramsay once and for all, talked about living in a better world. Even though sleep was still a long way off, they were already dreaming.

CHAPTER NINE
BITTEN

It was morning again at the Hive. The scene played out exactly as it had every sunrise since Ramsay ruled over the garden: the dark, empty corridors; Croda, the purple-robed cricket, gliding toward the throne room; flickering torchlight; side-stepping guards; and little white cocoons stuck on Ramsay's web. Once more, the prophet knelt as Ramsay descended to take his throne.

"Yesterday you told me the battle belongs to him who fights closest to home. What words of warning or wisdom have you brought for me today, my prophet?" said Ramsay with a trace of anxiety.

"You are wise to remember the visions previously given to you." Croda fell silent—a sure sign he brought a revelation Ramsay would find pleasing.

Ramsay knew the cricket's tells well, and he was happy to flatter the prophet who enjoyed keeping him in suspense when news was good: "If I am wise, it is because I have been enlightened by the words you bring. Now tell me, what is today's message about?"

"Victory," the cricket wheezed. "After the battle's waged and the fight is done, how will we know who has won? One blinded, whose vision's gone, will be the first to see the victorious one."

Ramsay hummed with satisfaction. "This is a good word. If my blind prophet was on hand when the rebels make it to the Hive, we can ensure that you will be the first to share in my triumph. Surely that is what is meant by this prophecy, is it not?"

"Further word I have not received."

"Very well, good and faithful servant. You may take your leave." Before the prophet had reached the stairs, Ramsay called for his guards. "Assign two guards to stand watch over my prophet from this moment forward," ordered Ramsay. He was taking no chances that something could happen to Croda to make him unavailable the day he confronted the rebel leader face to face.

***

The Beesleys rose early the next morning. They wanted to go to the market but thought it would be too dangerous if the spiders were still looking for them. They agreed to wait a day and then one of them would sneak into Diterra to gauge if it was safe for them to be in public again.

With that issue settled, their talk returned to Waverly's history lesson from the night before. They wondered aloud what it would have been like to have seen the Queen and lived in her garden when there was no Dung Heap or being afraid or losing parents.

Oliver asked, "Do you think things could ever go back to the way they were?"

"We can't undo what's been done," said Waverly, fairly certain Oliver was talking, at least in part, about their parents again.

"Waverly's right," said Ben. "There's no undoing what Ramsay has done, but the Queen could still save us from him."

"But if she didn't come back when the bugs wore bee coats and fought the spiders so she could return, why would the Queen come back now?" asked Oliver.

"That gives me an idea." said Ben. "Wait here!" He tore out of the house, leaving Waverly and Oliver staring at each other.

A few seconds later they heard Mrs. Galway holler, "Get out of my yard!"

A second after that, Ben rushed back into the house carrying three yellow leaves from Mrs. Galway's yard, one of which had been splattered with the indigo used on her house. "I spilled some paint on this leaf yesterday," said Ben. "It reminded me of something, but I couldn't figure out what exactly. You just helped me remember." He dropped the leaves on the floor and fetched the little bit of indigo they had left. On the back of each leaf, he painted three thick purplely-black lines.

"What are you doing?" Oliver asked.

"Maybe the Queen's ready to come back but is waiting for someone to prepare the way for her return. I thought one way to do that is to bring back the bee coats after all this time," said Ben. "So I'm making some bee coats for us."

"Whoa, whoa, whoa," said Waverly. "I'm all about letting her know we want her back and all, but there's got to be some other way. Wearing bee coats is crazy; remember what happened to the last bugs who did that."

"We'll only try them on inside the house," answered Ben. "It's not like the spiders would find out."

This sounded enough like a compromise for Waverly. Oliver, however, needed no persuading whatsoever. After the paint dried, everyone picked a leaf, poked out arm and wing holes, and slid them on like jackets.

"Wow!" said Oliver. "Waverly you look amazing! And you look really tough, Ben."

"Yours makes you look taller, Oliver," said Waverly, smiling at her elated little brother. "I'm serious."

"No spider would mess with us while we were wearing these," said Ben. "I really wish I could see what we looked like together."

"There's still some dew on the grass," said Waverly as she looked outside. "We could probably see our reflection in one of the drops."

Abandoning their pledge to wear the jackets only inside, they hastily flew out their door to get a look at themselves. Standing before a row of dew drops dangling from blades of grass, they posed and admired their reflections in the beads of water. Standing side by side, they were convinced that anyone seeing them for the first time might honestly mistake them for real bees.

Soon they were all zipping through the sky, admiring each other's coats in the sunlight and imagining themselves doing the things bees would have done—saving a broken-winged butterfly, chasing spiders out of the garden, bowing before the Queen to welcome her home.

They were so fully immersed in their make-believe world that they did not notice Chip and Todd coming up the hill. "What are you weirdos doing?" asked Chip, looking less muddy than the last time they saw him.

Startled by the sound of Chip's voice, the Beesleys returned to earth so quickly it was as though their jackets had turned to stone. The Lockwoods' intrusion was a sobering reminder that dressing up as bees was an audacious and dangerous act that could land them in serious trouble.

"Just flying around," said Oliver. They quickly shed their jackets and tossed them inside their house. "What's it to you?"

"We want a rematch," stated Chip bluntly, failing to acknowledge the strange fact of their urgently discarded clothing.

"Whenever you want to race, we're ready," answered Ben.

"Right now," said Chip, "but on one condition: all three of you have to race this time."

"Fine by me," said Waverly, emboldened by getting away with donning the outlawed coats.

Like the night before, both teams selected a suitable racing leaf and carried it to the top of the hill. The Lockwoods' leaf was much sleeker than the maple leaf they picked the first time around. The Beesleys devised a strategy to accommodate a third rider. Oliver would start out sitting in the middle of the leaf with his hands on the steering stem. Waverly and Ben would handle the running start and jump on next to Oliver, locking their arms together around his back.

Everyone agreed to let Todd start the race as the Lockwoods insisted they should have the honor and Todd was less likely than Chip to cheat by counting off unreasonably fast or softly or some such nonsense. The Beesleys got off to a better start than the night before, and the teams were neck and neck as they crossed the main road. But a strange thing happened in the meadow. With about a quarter of the race to run, Waverly looked over to see Chip steer the Lockwoods' leaf to the side of the hill as they slowed drastically.

"That's odd," she reported to her team. "Chip and Todd look like they're stopping."

Ben looked back to see for himself. "It's a trap!" he yelled. "Stop it! Stop the leaf!"

Ben and Waverly put their hands and feet out to the side dragging them against the ground, but they were going too fast to stop before they hit the earthen ramp. Oliver tried to steer them to the side of the ramp by jerking the stem hard to the left.

It almost worked. Instead of hitting the ramp head-on at full speed, they were skidding sideways when they launched into the sky. The leaf flipped over, scattering its riders. Ben plunged straight down, hitting the hard ground below and rolling to the edge of the pond. Waverly catapulted high into the air while Oliver, tumbling head over heels, shot out in a straight line beneath her. He smacked into the lower corner of a web anchored between two trees and came to a sudden, lurching stop. Oliver hung upside down with his back pinned to the sticky netting. A second later, Waverly landed face first on the web a few inches above Oliver.

"Waverly! Are you okay?" shouted Oliver, looking up at her between his feet.

Waverly tried to push away from the web, but it was no use. "I'm stuck," she answered.

"Me too," said Oliver.

"I think we're in a spider web."

"Well of course you are," another voice interrupted. "Dear me, you look positively stunned. You didn't think we'd give up so easily, did you?"

77

It was Noth. He hoisted himself up and crawled out onto the web toward Waverly and Oliver as he spoke. Scores of webs suddenly sprung up around the pond, each strategically built to make an escape next to impossible. No fewer than two hundred spiders came out of hiding and circled around the three little flies. The spiders were taking no chances their trap would fail to catch its prey.

"Let them go!" demanded Ben, who in spite of his hard landing was pulling himself to his feet. Menacing spiders crowded around him on all sides.

"Who is this who speaks to me as though I am a slave obliged to his commands?" asked Noth.

"I'm Ben Beesley, and those are my friends on your web; you must let them go." At that moment a small band of spiders came running down the hill clutching the bee coats they retrieved from the Beesleys' house.

"Ben," said Noth as he walked across his web to Waverly, "you recognize those, don't you? Interesting coats and your friends were wearing. Fans of bees, are we? Supporters of the ene-mies of Ramsay? If you were hoping to lead a revolution, you're off to a lousy start with your only two followers stuck in my web." He put the sharp tip of his foreleg in the middle of Waverly's back.

"Leave her alone!" shouted Ben.

"Leave her alone," snickered Noth. "She's on my web after having openly supported rebellion and broken dozens of Ramsay's rules in the last two days, and you have the nerve to tell me to leave her alone. I suppose you would rather I knit the chubby one a sweater than eat him."

Half amused and half appalled by Ben's brazenness, Noth continued, "Tell me—and you only get one chance—where is it you came from and what are you doing here. Tell me that, and I might let your little pals go."

"I'm just here to help my friends."

"Have it your way," said Noth, stepping onto Waverly's back. She disappeared underneath the spider's body. "I'm actually glad you decided not to cooperate."

"Look, I'll tell you anything you need to know. If it's me you want, I'm right here. Why don't you take me and leave them alone?" He held up his hands as if to surrender. Two burly spiders grabbed Ben's arms and pinned them behind his back.

"You see," explained Noth, "It's not really me who wants you; it's Ramsay. I am telling you this because I don't want you to mistake what I do next for an act of mercy, because it's anything but. Because if it was up to me, I wouldn't even send these two to the Dung Heap—Chubs here would be my dinner tonight." Noth extended his foreleg and tapped Oliver's foot, sending chills through his little body. "However, Ramsay wants to see you face to face. But he wants you to come to him ... on your own.

"Ramsay thinks you're dangerous. He thinks you're a rebel. His concern is that if we let you go, there's nothing to keep you from recruiting your army and showing up at the Hive when you're ready to destroy it. So we thought we needed to give you a real good reason to go see Ramsay soon.

"Based on your willingness to bark demands at me on behalf of your little friends when you're surrounded by hundreds of spiders, I think I know what will do the trick. So I will let your friends go ... but not before I give them something to remember our time together."

"I promise you," pleaded Ben, "I'll go see Ramsay on my own. I'll leave right now. You don't have to do anything more to convince me to go."

Noth swung back to the ground on a strand of spider silk tethered to the web. He shuffled toward Ben as he said, "I find that hard to believe coming from someone who keeps company with these capable liars. Given your history, a guarantee is essential."

With that, Noth stared into Ben's face, stood on his back legs, raised his arms and barked, "Release Lipo and San!"

On Noth's command, several spiders on each side of the web hoisted two wooden cages into the air. When the cages were raised level with the web, the handlers of the Malicious Poison Spiders released the locks and jumped back as the gates swung wide open. Two wiry spiders with wild eyes peaking out through a tangle of matted red hair burst out of the cages. They were aggressive and quick and made unintelligible grunts as they slobbered toward Waverly and Oliver who let out terrified, helpless screams.

"Please," begged Ben, "You don't have to do this! I'll go see Ramsay!"

"It's a little late for please. Besides, I know I don't have to do this," said Noth with a sick grin on his face. "I want to do this."

Even with her face pinned to the web, Waverly could sense San was rapidly closing in on her. She screamed even louder and struggled futilely to pull herself free, exhausting every muscle in her body.

San stepped onto her back and leaned his head down close to hers. His breath was hot and rancid, and she felt his drool splash her neck. Rearing his head back slightly, San opened his mouth to reveal the long, venom-drenched fangs he was about to plunge into

Waverly's neck. He snapped his head down and bit her hard. Waverly's cries of terror now flooded with pain.

"No!" Ben screamed, struggling vainly to free himself from the spiders' grasp.

Oliver too was yelling at San, begging him to leave Waverly alone when Lipo crept into his line of sight. Oliver tried to kick him but was so ensnared in the web his leg didn't move at all, which only showed everyone just how vulnerable he was.

Lipo crawled on top of Oliver and in an eerily efficient manner, without reservation or thought, sunk his teeth into Oliver's neck under his left cheek. Oliver let out an agonized shriek.

After Lipo and San had struck their targets, their handlers ventured onto the web carrying long sticks with a loop on the end and slipped the rope around their necks. Lipo and San shook violently to break free. Though the handlers struggled to keep their grip, they forced the flailing spiders back into their cages.

Waverly and Oliver were left crying on the web. Ben turned to Noth and demanded, "What have you done to them?"

"Lipo and San merely provided the guarantee I needed. They're what's known as Malicious Poison Spiders. Unlike normal spiders, their venom is a slow-acting poison that ravages their victims' brains. While their bite is always lethal, the venom takes two full days to run its course.

"When we let your little friends down, they'll feel a burning sensation at the site of the wound and be incredibly tired. They'll wake after a short sleep and feel perfectly healthy. But that feeling, like so many feelings, is deceptive. They might think they narrowly escaped, but the poison will have only begun to do its work. Slowly, relentlessly, it will overwhelm them.

"The effects are almost imperceptible at first. Their memories will fade, their minds will dull, and their thinking grow muddled. Gradually, they'll lose the ability to control their muscles. The changes are subtle—a slight twitch, an unsteady walk. They'll have difficulty speaking as their tongues swell inside their mouths and become increasingly difficult to control.

"The changes will make them frustrated and afraid, all the while the poison marches quietly on, attacking their brains. Soon they'll be so addled by the poison they won't be able to remember their own names or to think the thoughts necessary to fly, walk, or even stand. Although their mouths will make noise, you won't understand a single word they utter, and if you could, you would weep bitterly with the realization their words were merely spit from their mouths out of habit and free of any meaning.

"Finally, all that remains will be the shell of their body, standing empty as a gutted house. No thoughts, no words, no movement. Their hearts will forget how to beat, their lungs forget how to breathe, and then, they die." Noth clearly enjoyed the intricate details of suffering.

"That's what happens ... unless you see Ramsay. It's his garden and only he has the power to free them from this curse. Make no mistake, their lives are in your hands—Ramsay won't even consider helping them unless it's you who brings them to him."

As Noth finished his speech, the handlers of San and Lipo pulled Waverly and Oliver from the web and ingloriously dumped them into the muddy pond below. Ben rushed in to pull them out of the knee-deep water as the spiders trickled carelessly past on their way back to Diterra. Surrounded by hundreds of abandoned spider webs, Ben knelt over his wounded friends while their jackets tumbled away on the breeze.

With the spiders gone, Ben helped Waverly and Oliver to their feet, wrapped his arms around them, and struggled to lead them back to their house. Once inside, Ben cleaned their wounds and laid them on the soft floor. He knew he could not let them sleep long, for they did not have much time—less than two days to reach the Hive. He sat on the ground between them and thought about the journey ahead. Then, holding their hands in his, Ben wept for his friends.

CHAPTER TEN
FIGHTING

Ben composed himself and left his friends to rest while he made preparations for their journey. If Noth's depiction of the effect of the poison was accurate, Ben reasoned he would need the cart to transport Waverly and Oliver at some point. So he filled it with apples, enough to feed the three of them for at least two days. Then he shoved a blanket into the cart's net and hung a couple of water-filled shells from its handles.

Next Ben took Pupa to Mrs. Galway's to ask her to keep him for a while. She agreed. She even seemed excited at the prospect of having regular company for a change.

When Ben returned to the house, Waverly and Oliver were awake and rubbing their sore necks. He sat by Waverly's feet and said, "I'm glad you're awake."

"I'm not glad about anything," replied Waverly, her trembling voice rife with anger. "If they had any decency they would have done us in or just left us alone. Making us their slaves is humiliating enough, why did they need to make us their play things too? If that's all we are and all we'll ever be in this stupid garden, what's the point in fighting to hold on to that?"

"The point? The point is you were made for so much more than that," replied Ben. "And you're worth fighting for."

The evident affection behind Ben's words caught Waverly by surprise. She quickly recovered and with a somber face countered, "You heard about what happened to the bees Ramsay invited to the Hive. This is just another one of his traps, and he is using us as the bait to get you there."

"That may be," said Ben, "but if I want to help you, I have to see Ramsay. I know it's risky, but it's our only chance."

"No! There's no 'our.' It's my only chance and it's Oliver's only chance, but it's not yours. You can save yourself now by just walking away."

"Look the spiders had all three of us, but for some reason they left me alone. Maybe it is just some sick game, but as long as they're playing a game that leaves us even a chance of winning, then I have to play."

"That's where you're wrong. The whole thing is set up to guarantee you lose. Don't you see the only way you can win is if you refuse to play? If you go to the Hive, Ramsay will destroy all three of us, and I won't let you sacrifice yourself like that."

"But I have to!"

"You don't have to! You don't owe us anything."

"That's not it," said Ben. "I know you didn't expect anything in return for saving me. I have to do this because I love you two. You're my family, and you're worth fighting for."

Waverly fell silent. Such love from someone who had been a stranger to her a few days ago overwhelmed her. She knew at that moment she had lost the argument—Ben was not going to give up on them as long as he lived. He was indeed their very true friend and, even for flies like Waverly and Oliver, it was hard for them to believe they could be loved that much.

With tears in her eyes, Waverly threw her arms around Ben and gave him a kiss on the cheek. "Thank you," she whispered.

Oliver, who had been sitting forlornly on the floor, rose up and stretched his arms around both of them and said, "Mrs. Galway was right, Ben. You remind me of a bee too. And if you're going to Ramsay's Hive, then I'm going with you ... for as long as I can." In a puffed-up voice he added, "Besides, you'll probably need my help."

With that, the Beesleys said goodbye to the only home they had ever known, almost certain they would never see it again. But, there was no time to be sentimental—they had less than two days to make it to the Hive. Waverly and Oliver ran out their front door, grabbed the handles of the cart, and set off down their hill.

"Wait," said Ben, "let me get that."

"As long as I still can," Waverly said, "I'm pushing it. You can do it all you want when I'm done."

Oliver smiled, and Ben knew better than to argue. At the main road, for the first time in their lives, they turned left instead of right. Rather than traveling to Diterra, against all their instincts and common sense, they headed toward the Hive.

***

After nearly an hour, the flies crested a hill to see a mosquito and two red millipedes walking toward them on the path. The millipedes' agitation made it clear the mosquito was an unwelcome companion. It only took a moment to learn why.

"Oh, come on," hollered the mosquito, "all I said was 'you're not that fat.' You need to focus on the positive—sure, you're fat, but it's not like you're *that* fat. It's a compliment!"

"That's it!" yelled Mr. Millipede. "I've had it! Get out of here! We were enjoying a nice, quiet walk until you came along and ruined it. Lousy mosquito!"

"I have a name you know! Look, I understand it gets hard to remember names—old age will do that—but here's a trick to help ..."

"I don't want to remember your name!" cried Mr. Millipede. "I want to forget that I met you! And I want you to leave us alone!"

"Oh, I get it. Don't think I don't know what's going on here. These flies come along, and suddenly you're too good to be seen talking to a mosquito!"

The flies stood dumbfounded as this scene played out before them.

"That's quite enough." Mr. Millipede said. "Good day!"

"Have it your way." Floyd allowed the millipedes to pass. As the last segment of Mr. Millipede's long body went by, Floyd stealthily landed on his back. With a dirty hand he wiped the tip of his long proboscis, his straw-like stinger, before plunging it down onto the millipede's backside. Floyd, however, could not break through Mr. Millipede's thick, armor-like skin and instead bent his proboscis in six different places.

Mr. Millipede was blissfully unaware of the fact he had been attacked, leaving Floyd to try once more. Unfazed, Floyd smoothed out his stinger by pulling on it with four of his legs. Then he leaned over Mr. Millipede's side to where his protective skin turned soft and, this time, successfully bit him.

"Owww!" squealed Mr. Millipede, curling into a ball so his head now pressed against his own rear end. He found himself face to face with Floyd, who was dangling in the air, his proboscis still stuck in the millipede's side. "If you don't let go of me right now, you won't like what happens," said Mr. Millipede with stern restraint.

Floyd whined, "But I only need a little blood. When you tighten up like this, I can't get any."

"You have one second to let go."

"Just one little sip ..." Before he could finish, a vapor rose off the millipede's body, enveloping Floyd and misting his eyes. He fell to the ground instantly.

With Floyd lying in a heap, Mr. Millipede unrolled and said, "Come on, honey. Let's get out of here." Stepping to the side of the road, Mr. Millipede's legs turned into a blurry whirl as he frantically burrowed a hole in the earth.

Before disappearing into the ground behind her husband, Mrs. Millipede stopped to scold Floyd: "Honestly! It's bugs like you who make it so we can't go out anymore." A second later she was gone.

Though he couldn't open his eyes, Floyd managed to yell in the direction where the millipedes had been: "It's bugs like you who make this garden reek, you ugly red gas bags! If you smelled any worse, these flies would be swarming all over you!"

"Hey, leave us out of it," said Oliver.

"Are they gone?" asked Floyd.

"Yes."

"Good." Floyd unleashed a wretched scream as he flitted about, fiercely rubbing his eyes.

"Are you okay?" asked Waverly.

"Okay? I'm in agony! It burns. It really, really burns. You gotta do something!"

"It's supposed to be every fly for himself around here," Waverly whispered to Oliver and Ben, correctly implying that nobody would blame them for leaving the mosquito on his own. "Still, we can't leave him like this."

"You're right," said Oliver. "The bees would have helped an injured bug, no matter how annoying he was ... or is."

"All right," Ben said, "I'll try to grab a hold of him so he doesn't hurt himself flying around blindly. You two get our water."

Waverly and Oliver fetched the water buckets from the cart, keeping their eyes on Ben and Floyd as the mosquito collided head first with a low lying tree branch. "Ouch! Watch where you're going, jerk face!" Instinctively, he punched the branch. Now his fist hurt too.

As Floyd clutched his hand, Ben flew underneath him, grabbed his ankles and tried to pull him to the ground. Floyd resisted, kicking at Ben's head.

"I'm not trying to hurt you," said Ben, who had nearly returned Floyd to earth in spite of his resistance.

Waverly and Oliver rushed toward them with buckets in hand.

"Don't think I won't go down without a fight," yelled Floyd, flapping his wings wildly and still kicking at Ben.

"You were punching a tree! I'm trying to help you." Without saying another word, Floyd thrust his proboscis at Ben, narrowly missing only because Ben dodged at the last second. Not wanting to give Floyd another chance, Ben shouted, "Throw the water! Hit him with the water!"

Waverly and Oliver simultaneously tossed the contents of their buckets at Floyd. Waverly splashed the water right on Floyd's face while Oliver accidentally doused Ben. Both Ben and Floyd fell to the ground, the water on their backs made their wings stick together rendering them unable to fly.

"Ooooh. That feels sooo goood," cooed the mosquito as the water washed over his eyes. "Do you have any more?"

Waverly replied, "We'll get some. Hold on."

With their shell-buckets in hand, Waverly and Oliver shot up into the air to look for a refill. Seeing a muddy puddle about ten feet off the path, they swooped down with their containers outstretched to scoop up some water. As Waverly filled hers, a strange thing happened: her right arm twitched, causing her to drop the bucket.

"Are you all right?" asked Oliver, who knew Waverly to be very steady-handed.

"I guess so," she answered, "but my bucket sunk all the way to the bottom. I don't think I can reach it."

"I've got mine still. It will be good enough."

While flying back to Ben and Floyd, another strange thing happened. Oliver's left wing locked up, as though it was refusing to beat. He fell suddenly. A second later he regained control without having spilled too much water.

"Oliver, what happened?" asked Ben, whose wet antennae still clung to his face.

"I don't know what happened, but I'm fine ... I think." Oliver, not wanting to soak Ben again, hovered over Floyd and carefully poured the water over the mosquito's head.

While Floyd rolled about in the water groaning in relief, Ben fixed his concerned gaze on his friends. Waverly's twitching hand and Oliver's game wing provided the first proof that the poison in their bodies was as real and dreadful a thing as Noth made it out to be.

"I'm glad you're feeling better," Ben said to Floyd, "but we have to get going."

Floyd rinsed the mud off his face and asked, "What's the rush?"

"We have to tend to some urgent business on the other side of the garden," said Waverly, not fully trusting the mosquito with their secret.

"You're in luck because I know this garden from one side to the other better than anybody you'll ever meet," replied Floyd. "Tell me where you're going, and I'll tell you the absolute best way to get there. It's the least I can do."

"It's okay, we're going all the way to the other side," said Oliver, trying to be as vague as his sister. "We'll just take this path to get there."

"You could do that—if you want to go to Ramsay's Hive and take five days to do it." Their hearts sank. The flies exchanged glances as if to ask "did he really say five days?"

"That's it, isn't it?" said Floyd loudly. "You're actually trying to get to the Hive? No bug in his right mind goes to Ramsay's unless they're leading a rebellion. Then again, any one leading a rebellion against Ramsay isn't really in his right mind."

"Not so loud," said Ben. "We are trying to get to Ramsay's, but we're not looking to start an insurrection or anything."

"Sure," said Floyd, giving Ben a wink. "I catch your drift. Don't worry, I won't tell anybody. Secret's safe with me."

"What if we need to get there in less than five days?" asked Ben. "Do you know a faster route to the Hive?"

Floyd pointed to the top of a small mountain. "This path goes all the way around that mountain—that's why it takes so long. But you can get to the top of the mountain from here pretty easy. If you take this trail to the peak, cut through the cloud forest that's on top and come down the other side, you'll take two or three days off your trip." Floyd leaned in close and added in a hushed voice, "And you didn't hear it from me, but you might be able to find some willing recruits up there for that rebellion you guys aren't leading." Floyd gave one last wink and took to the sky.

When Floyd was out of earshot, Oliver asked, "What did he mean by 'willing recruits?'"

"He thinks we're leading a rebellion against Ramsay," answered Ben, "and some bugs on this mountain aren't too happy with the spiders either."

"Why don't we rebel?" wondered Oliver out loud.

"Who knows, maybe he'll leave us no choice," said Ben. "But for right now, we just need to worry about getting there. Let's go."

They pushed the cart up the mountainside. At the peak they found a dense, humid jungle that defied the seasons. Although it was autumn, the temperatures in the jungle were as hot as on the most sweltering summer day. Whereas most of the garden suffered through debilitating drought, the abundance of rain in the jungle nourished so many plants, they had to fight each other over precious sunlight. Tree branches were so entangled it was impossible to tell where one started and the other stopped. Plants gave up producing flowers to devote their energy to growing longer, sharper thorns. Vines strangled the life out of trees and plants alike with relentless diligence.

They entered the jungle on a lightly worn trail barely wide enough for the cart. Waverly and Oliver pushed back the overgrown weeds and vines so Ben could squeeze it through the narrow passageway they created.

After a few hours of trekking in this painfully slow manner, they needed to rest. They left the cart on the path and sat down in a small clearing they discovered near the edge of a steep cliff overlooking a valley. Below they could see hundreds of ants. Little red ants scurried all around the jungle floor, over mud piles, up trees, and across vines. To their great surprise, the ants appeared to be cooperating with each other.

The flies watched in amazement as the ants stayed in straight lines, followed orders, and carried little bits of wood and stone a great distance before dropping their cargo at the feet of other ants who used the materials to build roads and fortifications. Behind these ants were still more ants turning fallen branches into giant wooden catapults.

"Can you imagine what Diterra would look like if flies worked together like that?" asked Waverly.

"Or the whole garden for that matter," said Oliver. "The spiders would be scared to death if they saw this!"

At that moment, a horn blared somewhere down below. Instantly, the ants dropped what they had been doing and scattered. Some climbed on top of the contraptions they had built and started loading them with rocks. Others picked up sticks and stones and formed a straight line stretching out across the entire width of the valley. Still others disappeared into the jungle's thick vegetation.

Alarmed by the combative posture of the ants, the flies dropped onto their bellies to be hidden from view and crawled to the edge of the cliff to keep an eye on the action.

"What are they doing?" whispered Oliver.

"I don't know," said Waverly. "Just watch."

From their perch they could see something in the distance rustling through the jungle. Whatever it was, it was coming closer and closer to the red ants.

"Did you see that?" asked Oliver. "What do you think it is?"

"Shhhh! Be quiet," ordered Waverly.

Next, they heard a series of loud creaking noises, which was followed by an even louder snapping sound. The leader ant stood in front of the long line of ants and called out, "Hold your fire," so loudly the Beesleys understood him clearly even from so far away.

"There's going to be trouble," said Oliver.

"There's going to be war!" said Ben.

Suddenly, dozens of rocks ripped through the air, rocketing toward the red ants at breathtaking speed. A few rocks landed harmlessly in the weeds while others ricocheted off trees. Others smacked into the large contraptions the red ants had built, sending wood splintering through the air. The rocks that struck the red ants, however, yielded gruesome results. A second after the projectiles stopped falling, thousands of black ants poured out of the distant jungle, charging at the red ants.

At the sight of the first black ant, the leader of the red ants screamed, "Fire!" and the red army readily obeyed. Their catapults flung heavy stones at the blitzing black army. For every empty thud, an indication the projectile missed its target altogether, the flies heard dozens of resounding 'thwacks' followed by a shower of agonized screams. Bugs were unquestionably being hurt; how many and how badly they shuddered to guess.

The long line of red ants charged head-first into the on-coming horde. Wielding their sticks as swords and stones as shields, the two sides collided in the middle of the jungle floor. As black and red ants fell grievously wounded to the ground, both sides fired their catapults again. This time the stones landed indiscriminately on the ants ensnarled in the fray. The flies, unable to stomach this spectacle any longer, turned away and trembled.

"I can't tand to watch," said Waverly.

"Why are dey doing dat to each oder?" asked Oliver.

Ben stopped them. "Did you hear yourselves?"

"What?" asked Waverly.

"'I can't tand to watch'," said Ben, repeating their words to them. "'Why are dey doing dat to each oder'."

"I didn't dound like dat," said Waverly, shocked to hear herself unable to say her words as they should be said.

"It's da poison," stated Oliver. "It's alweady working."

Waverly and Oliver turned away from the war around them only to be confronted by the one being waged within them. Fear and anger swelled within Waverly as she considered her own failing body. Her breathing quickened but she couldn't catch her breath. The jungle spun, her heart raced. She stood to walk away, but instead fell on her face.

CHAPTER ELEVEN
THE ANT

"What's wong wid her?" asked Oliver.

"I think she passed out," answered Ben. "We need some water."

"I know whe'e some is," said Oliver. "You tay he'e, I'll get it!"

Ben was uneasy letting Oliver go into the jungle alone without knowing for sure why Waverly had passed out. Before he could say anything, however, Oliver had pulled the bucket from the cart and was running back the way they came. After only a dozen or so steps, he completely vanished, leaving Ben waiting with Waverly.

Ben rolled Waverly onto her back and cradled her head on his knees. He talked to her and lightly tapped her face, hoping to get some sort of response. Within a minute, her eyelids began to flutter as she regained consciousness.

He was asking if she was all right when a strange red blur swinging on a vine zipped past them. Ben flinched. When the vine reached the peak of its upward swing, Ben discerned the red blur was actually a crazed fire ant. And only when the ant was swinging back toward them did Ben realize that the ant intended them harm.

Ben quickly laid Waverly's head on the ground and hopped to his feet. The ant pulled a rock out of the satchel hanging on his side. Ben tried to get out of his way but was too slow. The ant released the vine and, hurtling toward Ben, whacked him in the head with his weapon.

Blinded with pain, Ben fell to the ground behind Waverly. The ant landed in a crouch between them. With both flies incapacitated, he returned his weaponized rock to his satchel.

The muscular ant wore a black eye patch over his left eye, leaving his right eye to dart around vigilantly, ever on the lookout for an ambush. With the exception of two razor sharp pincers that protruded from his mouth like a pair of shears, his was a normal ant head. A couple of tattered old rags draped his body, remnants of what appeared to have been a uniform. On his head sat a brass-colored helmet with a large spike rising right out the top.

He calmly inserted a nubby cigar into the corner of his mouth as he tied Waverly's and Ben's hands behind their backs. With one swift motion, the ant hoisted them both off the ground, holding one of them on each of his shoulders. He carried them far off the path into the unknowns of the jungle.

Shortly afterwards, Oliver came running back with his bucket. He stopped short and looked around the jungle as though he hoped the flora itself would explain to him where Waverly and Ben had gone.

As he searched for clues regarding their disappearance, Oliver noticed a lone set of footprints tracked through the mud ahead of him. He traced those prints all the way back to the very spot where Waverly passed out. Whoever, or whatever, these prints belonged to could not have gotten very far. *If whoever made these prints took Ben and Waverly, he must know that I'm here too,* Oliver thought. *I better hide!*

Oliver set down the bucket and took to the air, flying up to a large tree off the path. He wobbled as he flew, but his bigger concern was the noise his wings made, which under the circumstances sounded as loud as a swarm of locusts to him. Once he landed, Oliver decided flying was too loud, too risky, and out of the question. Seconds after hiding himself, he heard a scarcely audible sound— like someone accidentally jostled leaves and quickly silenced them. A few moments later he saw the barbarous ant emerge from the jungle.

The red ant slunk over to where Oliver had been before he left the ground. He examined the discarded bucket and placed his feet on the very spot where Oliver had stood. Suddenly, the ant looked straight up, sniffed the air, and crept toward Oliver's tree. Closer and closer slowly he inched.

Don't panic, thought Oliver. *Think.* He looked up and noticed a small nut wedged between two branches, which mercifully gave him the idea he needed. The poison had not yet taken his ability to cling effortlessly to almost any surface, so he scurried straight up the side of the tree. By the time Oliver scaled high enough to dislodge the nut, the ant was standing underneath him.

When the ant looked up, Oliver was standing on a branch that completely hid him from view. Nevertheless the ant inhaled deeply through his nose and started climbing up the tree.

Oliver's heart pounded so hard he worried the ant could hear it. *If I just flew away, I'd be safe,* he thought. *But what about Waverly and Ben? He'll go back to wherever he took them at some point. If only I could follow him without getting killed in the process.* He looked up into the treetops. *I bet he couldn't see me if I was in the canopy.*

Making sure to stay hidden, Oliver threw the nut with all his strength. It clunked against a far off tree and fell to the ground. The ant spun his head toward the direction of the sound. He looked back up the tree and stared at the branch that held Oliver. He waited there a few seconds, then dropped straight down and raced toward the spot where the nut landed.

Oliver breathed a sigh of relief, which felt like the first time he remembered to exhale since he landed in the tree. Having put some space between himself and the ant, he hoped to make it to the tops of the trees without being detected. Oliver's plans were foiled when his arms twitched, causing him to lose his grip and slide down an inch before he caught himself.

The ant heard the incredibly faint sound of Oliver's legs scraping against the tree bark and turned around. In a panic, Oliver shot up into the tangle of branches, leaves, and vines at the top of the jungle where he was safely camouflaged. To his relief it appeared the ant had not spotted him before he disappeared into the tree tops.

Every now and then, the ant gazed up into the canopy, sometimes right at Oliver. But either his eyesight was not that good or he just could not figure out how to get his hands on Oliver, so he resumed his search on the ground. The ant scoured the jungle for a little less than two hours—a very precious two hours for a little fly with not much time. Oliver followed along as closely as he could, worrying how the poison might affect him next.

When the ant finally gave up his hunt, Oliver followed him back to a small clearing near a rock wall where a fire had burned the night before. Oliver saw his sister and his friend trapped inside a small cage, their feet and hands bound and gags tied over their mouths.

His relief at finding them alive was short-lived. *How am I ever going to get them out of there?* he wondered. For now he could only watch ... and think, think, think.

The red ant circled around the outside of the cage. He took off his helmet and wiped the sweat from his forehead with part of his old, tattered uniform. After placing the helmet back on his head, he grabbed the cage with two hands, pressed his face up against the bars and in a thick accent said, "My name is Colonel von Clausewitz." He paused dramatically and glared at Waverly and Ben through the bars. "I am a member of the Fire Ant Resistance Movement." Another pause and more glaring. "Now tell me who you are and who you're spying for?"

Ben tried to answer but found it hard to speak with a gag over his mouth. "Hmphfld."

"Don't lie to me!" Clausewitz reflexively yelled. Once he comprehended that Ben had not actually said anything, he jabbed his pincers into the cage.

Far above the forest floor, Oliver winced.

Clausewitz grabbed hold of Ben's bound hands and slid one of his pincers between the gag over his mouth and his cheek. Ben shivered when he felt the razor sharp pincer press against his face. Then suddenly, SNAP! The ant sliced through the gag, which slipped down Ben's back to the floor of the cage. Clausewitz snapped his pincers again and again next to Ben's head as he asked, "Now tell me—who are you and who are you spying for?"

"My name is B-Ben, Ben Beesley. And this is Waverly. We're not spying for anybody; we're just trying to get to Ramsay's Hive."

Clausewitz pulled Ben against the bars of the cage. "You really expect me to believe that?" he sneered.

"Yes."

"Why?"

"It's a long story."

"Believe me," said Clausewitz as he let go of Ben, "you're not going anywhere, anytime soon—might as well tell it."

"But we need to go. You see, some spiders bit my friends and told us only Ramsay could save them. If we don't get to the Hive, they'll die."

"You're lying."

"Everything I've said is the truth."

"Ramsay doesn't save; he only destroys. If you really think you're telling truth, then you've deceived yourself. You'll all die if you go to Ramsay's Hive."

"Maybe you're right about Ramsay. Still, making it to the Hive is their only chance. Now have you seen our friend?" asked Ben anxiously.

"The pudgy one, you mean?"

"His name is Oliver."

"Of course, I found him. He's locked away at another location. You can go on and on with this nonsense about Ramsay if you want, but Oliver told me everything already. Just thought I'd give you a chance to help yourselves by telling me the truth."

"Look, we don't have much time—you have to let us go."

"You know what I think?" questioned the ant without acknowledging Ben. "I think you were planning attacks on my brethren. Your friend told me how you've been working with the black ants."

"Now who's lying?" retorted Ben.

"Come on! You're black; they're black." Clausewitz's voice trembled with anger. "I'm sure you'd both want nothing more than to see the fire ants exterminated from this garden. Now tell me where you're planning on striking next, or your chubby little buddy gets it."

"You're crazy," Ben blurted out.

"Crazy!" screamed Clausewitz. "You don't know crazy. Crazy is war without end, your enemies always at your heels, one step ahead of annihilation every second of your miserable existence. And the only way to keep me from my loathsome fate is to ruin my enemies before they ruin me!" Clausewitz ripped open the cage and yanked Waverly out. After slamming the door shut and locking Ben inside, he tied Waverly to a stake. "It's my life or hers! Now, what's your army's next move?"

Oliver shook so terribly with fear for his sister, he nearly lost his grip. He knew he had to act soon.

She answered, "I don't even know what you'e tawking about. We don't have an awmy, and we don't want to huwt anybody—not even you."

Clausewitz picked a branch off the ground and held it in front of his face. He stared right at Waverly and his pincers snapped shut, slicing through the branch as easily as someone passing their hand through water. He drew closer to Waverly, cutting what was left of the branch in half with every step. When he ran out of stick to bite, he snapped his pincers together inches from her face and said, "You have one last chance to answer my question."

Oliver could wait no longer. He had left his sister and Ben's fate to this crazed ant for far too long already. While he was considering the best course of action, a sudden spasm caused him to tumble ingloriously out of the canopy instead. A few feet into his fall, Oliver smacked into a tree branch. He latched onto a stick that broke off in his hands, knocking a cluster of nuts from the tree. By flapping his wings madly, Oliver regained some control. With an eye on the ground and the stick in his hand pointed like a spear at Clausewitz, Oliver transformed his fall into a dive.

The nuts landed first, pelting the jungle floor or bouncing off the cage. One thunked Clausewitz in the head and got skewered on the spike of his helmet. Oliver followed by half a second and the tip of his branch jammed into the ground between Waverly and the ant. Despite the great impact of his landing, Oliver managed to hold on to the end of the stick, leaving him dangling in the air above the other bugs.

Though stunned, Clausewitz instinctively lunged at his assailant and broke the stick with his pincers. With his support cut out from under him, Oliver fell onto the ant's back and sent him crashing to the ground. Oliver sprang to his feet and, still holding what remained of the stick, ran to the cage. *I gotta get Ben out before that ant gets up,* he thought.

Oliver's wishful thoughts grossly underestimated the incredible quickness of Clausewitz. In a heartbeat, the Colonel was on his feet and on Oliver's heels. Oliver flew as fast as he could round and round the cage, trying to keep it between him and the ant, but Clausewitz was closing in rapidly. Waverly, who was still tied up, screamed for Clausewitz to leave Oliver alone. Meanwhile, Ben slipped free of his manacles and reached his hand through the bars, tripping the ant as he ran past.

Oliver felt the ant's hands brush against his back as Clausewitz tumbled. He realized he could never outrun the ant, and his best chance for helping Ben and Waverly rested on him trying to talk their way out. Oliver broke out of his circular flight pattern and positioned himself against the rock wall with his outstretched stick his only measure of protection. Clausewitz dusted himself off, then calmly approached his undersized and over-matched opponent.

"'Tay back," Oliver said. "I don't want to huwt you."

A malevolent grin filled Clausewitz's face, but before he could mock the little fly's defiant courage, a strange whizzing noise cut through the air. The whole jungle stopped to listen to the sound as it grew louder and lower. Clausewitz yelled, "Incoming!" and threw himself to the ground in front of the rock wall.

An errant rock, a misguided shot from one of the ant army catapults, barely missed Oliver before crashing against the rock wall with an explosive CLACK.

"GAAAHHH!" cried Clausewitz. The rock had broken into pieces, and one chunk fell on his right leg, pinning him to the ground.

Oliver threw down his stick and dashed over to free Ben and Waverly. Clausewitz, moaning in pain, futilely tried to free his leg. "The horror," he groaned, "the horror."

"We hab' to see ib he's otay," said Oliver. The flies drew near to see what they could do, but the ant lashed out, cussing and spitting at them.

Waverly said, "He's 'till too dansherous to he'p."

"Bees," said Oliver, "a'en't apraid of anyt'ing, 'member? Betides, he's onwy acting dat way 'cause he t'inks we'e going to huwt him." Worried the ant would not understand him, Oliver added, "Ben, tell him we won't huwt him."

"Relax," Ben said, "we don't want to hurt you." Clausewitz continued to threaten and thrash about. Ben knelt down just beyond the ant's reach and said, "You're going to hurt yourself even worse if you don't let someone help you."

"Help. Bah! I don't need help from you or anybody else."

"Do you want to stay under that rock for the rest of your life, or are you planning on gnawing your own leg off?"

"Neither." With that, Clausewitz pushed against the rock with all his strength, grunting, shaking, grimacing until his face turned impossibly red from all his straining. The rock didn't budge, so next he tried to free his leg by giving it a firm tug. Instead of finding freedom, he growled in pain and abruptly gave up. Clausewitz's shoulders sunk, his face drooped in defeat. "Fine," said the ant with his eyes downcast, "you win." He tossed his helmet at their feet.

"What's this?" asked Ben.

"That was my honor. It took many victories on many battlefields to earn that helmet. With that on my head, others had no choice but to respect and fear me. But that's all gone now. You've defeated me, which means it's your trophy. My shame is your glory."

Ben picked up the helmet, took two steps toward Clausewitz and put it back on his head. "I'm not interested in your shame. I want you to let me help you." Clausewitz protested, but Ben rebuffed him, reminding him the vanquished are at the mercy of the victors. At last the ant relented and accepted their assistance.

The rock was astonishingly heavy, and the three of them were not able to move it by hand. After much trial and error, they figured out how to use Oliver's stick as a lever to lift the rock just enough to free the ant's mangled leg. Even though Clausewitz winced every time they touched him, he nevertheless allowed them to bandage his leg with pieces of Oliver's stick used for a splint. Up on his feet again, the Colonel walked, if a little gingerly, on his makeshift cast.

Looking at his broken leg, a tear welled up in Clausewitz's good eye. Before it could roll down his cheek, the ant shifted his eyepatch to cover his watery eye. The eye long hidden under the patch appeared perfectly fine, even if it too was on the verge of shedding a tear. Clausewitz turned to hide his face.

"Youw weg wooked wike it huwt," said Waverly. "It's otay to cwy."

"It's not okay to cry!" the ant snapped back. "I am a warrior. My code is kill or be killed."

"Under your code," said Ben, "you should be dead. By giving you your life back when we had it in our hands, we invalidated your code. It doesn't have any power to shame you any more."

"You've done far more for me than I deserve," answered the humbled fire ant. "Believe me when I say, never in my life would I have thought of doing the same for you. So are you really going to Ramsay's Hive?"

The flies nodded.

"You wouldn't take my life, you refused my honor, but please accept my advice—if not as spoils of your victory, then as my meager attempt to repay your kindness. The first rule of war is to know the type of struggle you're waging. If you imagine it as anything other than it truly is, you've already lost. If he has drawn you to his Hive, make no mistake: he is at war with you. And with Ramsay, it can only be a fight to the death, for he knows no other way to fight. Though you're struggle is for life, know you can't win unless you're ready to fight to the death."

Unsettled by the ant's advice, the Beesleys thanked Clausewitz for his counsel, wished him well, and started back to fetch their cart.

"By the way," said Clausewitz, "to get to Ramsay's, you need to go over this rock wall and down the mountain. The path you were on just circles around the jungle."

The flies turned to look at the wall. When they turned back, Clausewitz was gone. In spite of his bad leg, he disappeared as suddenly as he had arrived.

Oliver said, "I can honestwy tay I'b neber met anyone wike him befo'e." They all nodded in agreement and walked toward the cart.

"I'm p'oud of you," said Waverly as she reached behind Oliver's back to give his shoulder a squeeze. "You we'e reawwy brabe. You sabed us."

Oliver blushed. "What e'se could I do?" he answered. "I'm just gwad ..." THUD.

Without warning, Oliver crumpled to the ground. His legs had simply given out from underneath him. His moment to play hero and bask in his friends' admiration was cut tragically short the poison's relentless assault on his body. Oliver's stumble in the jungle marked the beginning of a new phase in his and Waverly's decline. Walking and flying became increasingly difficult, and this stumble was only the first of many to come.

Oliver scratched his face in the fall. While it burned, his embarrassment was far worse than his pain. Ben helped Oliver to his feet, and knowing him well, spoke directly to his unexpressed thoughts: "It's okay, buddy. You don't have anything to be embarrassed about. I'm going to take care of you, no matter what. I'll do *whatever* it takes."

CHAPTER TWELVE
FALLING DOWN

Taking the route suggested by Clausewitz was more difficult than they imagined. The vegetation was so thick, Ben had to tie up the plants with nearby vines in order to clear a path. Twice his knots gave way, and the unruly weeds walloped the hapless flies in their faces. They pressed on. Many fallen trees lined this untrod path, at times leaving them no choice but for all three of them to lift their cart over the obstacle. Every time they did, Ben held his breath, fearing Waverly's or Oliver's body might betray them. When at last they made it to the rock wall, the relief they felt was as great as the effort expended in getting there.

They were talking through how to get the cart over the wall when Floyd came zipping through the forest toward them. "There you are! What a relief!" he exclaimed. "I thought you might have run into those crazy ants. Oh, I'm so glad you guys are all right. After you left, it hit me that I didn't tell you that you needed to climb over this wall for the shortcut to work."

"You dust 'membe'ed dat now?" asked Oliver, who was more than a little annoyed with the mosquito. "You nea'wy dot us tilled!"

"Huh? Seriously kid, you need to get the food out of your mouth when you talk—I can't understand a word."

"He said, 'You nearly got us killed'," explained Ben. "And he's right."

Floyd mumbled under his breath, "It's not like you won't all be dead in two days anyway."

"What did you tay?" asked Waverly.

"Oh ... ah ... I don't think you'll get there with this cart in two days anyway," said Floyd. "Admit it: it's slowing you up. If you don't ditch it, you won't get to the Hive in time."

"Without it, we might not be able to get there at all," said Ben. "If the poison does what the spiders said it would, they won't be able to fly much longer."

"But you don't even know how you'll get it over this wall. Think of how much time you're wasting. The sun will set soon, and you haven't made it that far from Diterra."

"If you'd weabe us awone, we'd fidu'e it out," snapped Oliver as his knee inconveniently buckled. He caught hold of Ben to prop himself up.

"Awone? Seriously kid, not one word," said Floyd. "Are you speaking Cicada or something?"

"'If you'd leave us alone, we'd figure it out'," Ben repeated. "And he's right again. Now if you'll excuse us."

"Fine, fine," grumbled Floyd, "I'll get out of your way." He flew to the top of the rock wall and sat on its edge looking down at them.

With Floyd out of the way and as quiet as they could hope him to be, they turned their minds to getting the cart over, under, around, or through the wall. This was the type of puzzle Waverly usually excelled at, but in this instance she couldn't think clearly. She recalled a time she had helped her dad hoist something heavy over a fallen log by using ropes, but the details of what they had done escaped her no matter how hard she tried to remember.

"Tick, tock," taunted Floyd. "Is it me, or is it getting dark?" Indeed the sun had begun its retreat over the horizon.

The flies glared at Floyd. Their frustration with him melted away when the dozens of thick branches hanging over his head caught Waverly's eye and jogged her memory in just the right way. She had Ben tie vines together to be used as a long rope. They secured the vines underneath the cart and ran them up over a large tree branch. Following Waverly's instructions, Ben ran the vines under the cart again, and back over the branches. When they finished, they had made a load-lightening pulley system.

Ben gave the vine a gentle tug, and the cart went high into the air. Seeing he could manage its weight by himself, he asked Waverly and Oliver to fly up to Floyd. They looked at Ben like he was crazy but did as he requested. At least they tried to. To their dismay, their little wings beat so erratically they could no longer fly. Instead they fluttered back to the ground, where they stared at Ben as if to ask, "Now what?"

"I was worried about that," said Ben stroking his chin. "You'll have to ride up on the cart." Waverly and Oliver climbed aboard and held on tight. A few minutes later, the cart and all the flies were over the wall and back on solid ground. Ben untied the vines from the tree to set the cart free.

From where they stood, they could see more of the garden at one time than they ever had before, and it looked unusually beautiful in the fading daylight. The sun setting behind them cast long shadows and lent a lustrous red tint to the graying plants. The valley below was bordered to the north and south by more mountains and to the east by a placid lake that stretched out as far as they could see.

The heat of the jungle retreated into their memories as a cool autumn breeze rushed over them. The relief they felt at having surmounted the rock wall was short-lived once they realized they had merely exchanged one hardship for another: the only way down to the valley was by descending the impossibly steep mountain they found themselves atop.

"A little steep, ain't it?" asked Floyd. "Good luck getting down that with your little cart. Look, I got to run, but it was nice seeing you. We'll have to do it again some time, preferably not at Ramsay's Hive!"

As he rose to his feet, Floyd added, "Let me leave you with one last piece of advice. You might run into some termites in the valley. If you get hungry or need a place to rest, let them help you." Then Floyd took to the air, and the flies watched him drift away until he became a speck on the horizon.

With Floyd gone, they began their descent along a stony path that zigged and zagged its way down the mountain. Ben cautiously maneuvered the cart around each turn, and Waverly and Oliver walked behind him so he could break their fall in case they tripped. However, when Oliver stumbled and knocked Waverly into Ben from behind, Ben slipped on the pebbles underfoot. He lost hold of the cart and it careened out of control, stopping only when it wedged between two rocks. If not for those rocks, the cart would have disappeared over the side of the mountain and been smashed on the ground below. The thought he had come so close to losing it left Ben mortified.

Spotting a vine still tied to the underside of the cart, Ben cinched the loose end around his waist to ensure the cart would never get away from him again. But that only addressed part of the danger: Waverly and Oliver still needed a safer way to get down. Using a sharp-edged rock, Ben sawed off many of the pine cone's wood-like scales from the top of the cart, leaving a large open space. Next, he took the two largest scales he had cut and turned them into two seats by gluing them over the open space with the sticky sap oozing from the cone.

When the sap had hardened he called out, "Your chariot awaits." With his help, Waverly and Oliver climbed up and took their seats. Before resuming their journey, Ben fashioned seat belts for them over protests that he was babying them. "Just being safe— I'm not about to do you in myself," he said in his defense.

About half way down the mountain, the terrain started to change. The winding path gave way to a straight, wide-open swath of rutted soil. The rugged boulders were replaced with small, slippery stones that made walking that much more treacherous. To complicate matters, the sun had set, and dark clouds blocked the stars and the moonlight.

"I'm t-told," said Waverly.

"I'm hung'y," added Oliver, "and sweepy too."

"We've got food and a blanket under the cart. Just a second." Ben set the cart down and reached his hand into the net for some fruit but felt none. "That's odd. I know I packed apples." He got down on the ground to see for himself what happened to their cargo.

"Our food is gone," said Ben. "We may have to find those termites Floyd told us about after all. I'll get you the blanket."

He stretched out to grab the blanket, but it was just beyond his reach. He scooted closer to the cart until his head pressed against it. With his arm extended as far as it could go, his hooked fingers brushed the edge of the blanket. Ben rocked forward and snagged it. Before he could say "got it," it dawned on him that his head was no longer touching the cart and the blanket was coming out of the net before he started pulling his arm back.

"NO!" he shouted. Ben grasped for a handle, but the cart was already out of reach. Dropping the blanket at his feet, he took hold of the vine around his waist with both hands and gave it a firm tug. But instead of the cart stopping, he started down after it. The rope pulled tight and yanked him off the ground as the blanket wrapped around his legs. Somehow, he landed standing up, his blanket-covered feet sliding over the tiny stones and loose dirt.

As the cart continued to pick up speed it got harder and harder for Ben to stay upright since the impact of every little bump was magnified the faster they went. The cart bucked and rattled more and more wildly until its front wheels rolled over a big stone that launched it into the air. Waverly and Oliver rose out of their seats at the height of the cart's arc and only their lap belts kept them from flying out.

Ben was heading toward the same stone and spread his legs apart hoping to straddle the rock and save his knees from serious damage. Even though his legs missed the rock, the blanket caught on the stone and sent Ben tumbling just as the rope around his waist tightened again and pulled him up in the air behind the cart. Ben heard Waverly and Oliver screaming as he flipped end over end before landing with a belly flop.

He hit the ground so hard he bounced into the air again and did another flip. This time he saw the stone he had tripped over rumbling down the mountain behind them. "Crikey!" As he cut through the air, he reached down to pull the blanket clear of his feet.

At the highest point in his upward bounce, Ben felt the merciless tug of the rope once more and knew he would be returned, rather painfully, to earth. He desperately flapped his wings in a futile effort to counter the cart's momentum. He smacked against the ground and was dragged over the rocky soil, every now and then getting popped into the air when the cart rolled over a rock.

Just when he thought he could not take anymore, the cart bounced into the air yet again. Instead of another hard landing, this time Ben took the blanket in both hands and it swelled up like a parachute. Not only did it save him from another painful fall, it was slowing down the cart. Just in time too, for they had nearly reached the valley floor where there were all kinds of things to crash into.

But slowing down came with its own challenges. Ben looked beneath him and saw the rock that had first taken him out now leading the charge of a small avalanche that was rapidly gaining on the cart.

"Waverly! Oliver!" he shouted. "If you can hear me, lean to your left! Lean to your left!"

Waverly and Oliver were relieved to hear from Ben again for they had no idea what was happening behind them, but it did not sound good. Obediently, they leaned hard to their left, veering out of the path of the avalanche that rumbled past them as they came to a stop.

They watched the rocks crash into a gigantic brown edifice, which looked like someone had frozen a fire and coated it with mud. The building had a broad round base that came to a narrow point at the top, with a dozen or so tall spires shooting off in all directions, haphazardly stretching to the sky. Its very existence was a defiance of gravity. The largest stone rammed its way inside as the others bounced off the front of the mound. The shaft of light that shot out of the hole left by the rock nearly blinded the flies.

As Waverly and Oliver squinted into the brightness, Ben glided in with his parachute still in hand and landed on top of them. He propped himself up and breathlessly uttered, "Maybe ... we can take ... a short break." With that, Ben passed out on their laps.

Waverly and Oliver sat motionless in their seats with Ben draped over them like a blanket. They were glad to still be alive after their death defying descent but feared Ben might not have been so lucky.

CHAPTER THIRTEEN
THE MOUND

Waverly and Oliver carefully rolled Ben off their laps, fearful of the consequences their friend would suffer if he fell from the cart. By flipping him over they were able to better survey his injuries: two black eyes, a huge knot rising out of the middle of his forehead, what looked like a broken arm, clumps of gravel stuck in his chest, and scrapes, bruises, and cuts too plentiful to count.

"Do you tink he's a'ight?" asked Oliver, who was only modestly comforted to see his friend's chest rise and fall.

"At weast he's 'till bweaving," said Waverly. "We need to det him hewp."

Waverly and Oliver attempted to unfasten their seat belts, but untying Ben's overprotective knots proved far more difficult than they anticipated. Instead, Waverly slid down in her seat, wriggling from side to side until the belt passed over her head. Unfortunately, Oliver's belly would not allow him to do the same, so he pushed himself up, bending and twisting awkwardly until the belt worked its way down over his feet.

"I tink we need to take Ben intide," said Waverly. "It's faw too told to tay out hewe."

"But awen't you wowwied bout what's intide dat ting?"

"A wittle. But 'member—Fwoyd taid we'd find tewmites hewe who might hewp us. Maybe dis is whewe dey wibe."

"Wibe?" asked Oliver, who found it increasingly difficult to understand his sister.

"You know, dis might be da tewmite's home."

They decided to peek into the hole to see if there was anybody who could help them. Asking a stranger for anything went against all they had learned growing up in Diterra, but under the circumstances they had no choice. Their mistrust was still strong enough that they were not about to leave Ben alone on the cart as they approached the structure.

Oliver grabbed Ben's shoulders as Waverly picked up his legs, hoping to carry him at least a short distance. They got him off the cart, but Ben slipped through their fingers and dropped to the ground. Mortified by what they had done, Waverly and Oliver repeatedly apologized to Ben while they tugged at the vine around his waist.

"Would you like some help?" called a voice behind them as shadowy figures marched through the spotlight coming out of the mound.

Waverly and Oliver spun around to see twenty white insects with large heads attached to preposterously larger mouths and jaws. Most were examining the hole and the rocks scattered all around. Three of them, however, walked straight over to Waverly and Oliver.

"Oh, hi," said Waverly. "I tink we tould use a hand." Dropping Ben had thoroughly convinced them of their need for help—not to mention his—that they didn't even think about being frightened or suspicious, a customary response when meeting strange bugs for the first time in the garden.

"What a strange manner of speaking you have," said one of the white bugs.

Waverly and Oliver wanted to explain what had happened to them, but thought getting Ben the assistance he needed was more important so they simply nodded in agreement.

"Allow me to introduce myself," said the plumpest of the bugs, who wore a tiny crown on her head. "I am Queen Dalnatria-patrima, First Among the Termites, Sovereign of the Mound."

Did she say Queen? thought Waverly and Oliver. *How could that be? There can only be one Queen, and no one has seen her for years? And why would Ramsay put up with someone claiming to be Queen?* Nevertheless, she acted regally enough to convince them she was what she claimed to be. For two humble flies from Diterra, it was an honor to be in the presence of royalty.

They flies bowed, and Waverly said, "Bery pweased to meet you, youw highness."

"Ib you pwease Queen Dawna ... Dawnatwia ..." said Oliver, trying to pronounce the Queen's proper name properly.

"Please, your Majesty will suffice."

"Ib you pwease youw Majesty, my name is Owiber Beeswee, and dis is my sista, Waberwy Beeswee."

"Welcome to my Kingdom, Owiber and Waberwy," said Queen Dalna. "I wanted to be the first to greet you. It's the royal way, after all. You may stay with us as long as you wish. While you're here, what's mine is yours. But I have much urgent business to tend to, so I must be off. I leave you with my servants, Zimra and Ulli." Giving a little wink she added, "Leaving the work to your servants is also the royal way! Ta-ta."

As Queen Dalna walked back to the mound she said to Zimra and Ulli, "Make sure they get all they need and more. Remember, too much is not enough." The Queen retreated into the mound with half her entourage following close behind.

"Hello Waberwy and Owiber. My sister and I are here to take care of you," said Zimra. The sisters looked almost identical, both lean and pale, with Zimra standing a bit taller than Ulli. "If there is anything you need, anything at all, let us know. Your comfort is our priority and you certainly can't be comfortable standing here in the cold. Let's get inside."

"What 'bout our fwiend?" asked Oliver, pointing at Ben.

"I didn't even notice him," said Zimra. She walked toward Ben and looked him over. "Oooh, he is in bad shape, isn't he? No worries, though. We'll see to it he gets patched up and back on his feet in no time." She turned to the termites still lingering in front of the mound and clapped her hands. Four of them rushed over, picked Ben up, and effortlessly carried him inside. Waverly and Oliver followed close behind and, with assistance, made it into the mound. Once inside, the termites set to work patching up the hole.

The mound was the most sensational place Waverly and Oliver had ever been. They marveled at its pulsing lights, dazzling colors, the roar of thousands upon thousands of termites, and most wonderfully, the enticing aroma of food, glorious food. The place bombarded their senses, and they could scarcely take it in. They scanned the cavernous hall, following its walls all the way up to the impossibly high ceiling, which seemed to hover a mile above the ground. Their eyes fixed on a pair of enormous staircases that went up to the ceiling and spiraled along the walls all the way around the mound and back down to the floor.

Giant glowing signs hung at different points along the stairs and spelled things like, "Good Eats," "Roll the DICE!" and "Live Shows." Spacious platforms sat beneath the signs, each led to one of the many spires Waverly and Oliver had admired from the outside. Very few termites, however, actually used the stairs. Instead, they squeezed into the wooden elevators spread throughout the great chamber, riding the creaky lifts up to the platforms where they spilled out and disappeared into the spires.

In the middle of the hall, trapezes and tightropes had been suspended high above the ground. A spotlight shone on a termite performing one spectacular trick after another on a trapeze as the crowd sitting on rows and rows of bleachers below cheered his every move. The acrobat transfixed Waverly and Oliver. They cringed at every stunt, certain disaster would follow, and clapped in relief after every perfectly executed trick.

"I'm glad you like it," said Zimra. "The circus runs all night and day, but the performers do take fifteen minutes off once every week. We apologize for the inconvenience."

Oliver tore his gaze away from the circus act to look at Zimra. "Intonbenience? It's amading!" At that moment, he became aware for the first time that Ben was no longer with them. It made him nauseous to think he had been so easily distracted that Ben could be whisked away without him realizing. Oliver scanned the crowded room but saw only termites, thousands of them.

"Whewe'd you tabe our pwiend?" asked Oliver with panic in his voice. Zimra and Ulli stared at Oliver, uncertain of what he had said. Their blank expressions made him that much more fervent. "Our pwiend, Ben! Whewe is he?"

121

"Whewe's Ben?" asked Waverly.

"Oh, Ben," said Ulli, as though she had just deciphered a riddle. "He's in good hands. Look over there on the stairs." She pointed about a third of the way up the wall to their left where Ben was being carried up by the termites who brought him in from the outside. They stopped at a platform underneath a large lit sign that read, "Recovery Rooms Available."

Sensing Waverly and Oliver's apprehension, Ulli said, "Don't worry. They're taking him to a room where he can get some rest. They'll take good care of him."

"We should 'tay wit Ben," said Waverly, as she started toward the stairs. She was now hunched over, and her feet turned in toward each other. After only a few steps she stumbled.

Zimra got to Waverly before Oliver could and helped her to her feet. "I'm otay," said an embarrassed Waverly, leaning on Zimra and still trying to get to the stairs.

Oliver's feet also turned in, which caused him to trip too. Ulli reached out with surprising speed and caught him before he could fall.

"Clearly you two need of some additional assistance," said Ulli. She motioned to some termites dutifully stationed along the wall and instructed, "Bring the wheeled chairs we use for guests who've had a little too much, if you know what I mean."

After the servants dispersed, Zimra said, "Know what I think? All this worry over Ben can't be good for you. Let's give you a little break before we visit him. If you need a good night's sleep, we'll give you a soft, warm bed. Maybe it's a luxuriant mud bath you crave: we can take you to our spa in spire three. We've also got every kind of show imaginable at any time of day for your enjoyment. Or maybe you just need something to eat. That's it, isn't it? You need to visit one of our all you can eat buffets?"

The termites returned pushing wheel chairs. Waverly's eyes had been glued to the stairs where Ben had been but turned to look suspiciously at the chair. "It's all right," Zimra coaxed. "Let us take care of you to get you ready to take care of Ben."

"Well, otay," Waverly said, climbing into the chair with a little help. "But we p'obabwy tan't tay wong,"

"Nonsense," said Zimra. "You can stay as long as you like."

As Oliver settled into his chair he asked, "Did she tay aww I tan eat?" The phrase "all you can eat" had been running wild in his brain since Zimra uttered the words.

"And then some," answered Ulli flatly.

It had been a long time since their last meal, so Waverly and Oliver agreed to get something to eat first and then to take some food to Ben. Zimra and Ulli rolled them over to a bank of elevators along the outer wall. They plowed the chairs through a horde of termites and onto an elevator and rode it up to a platform with two orange signs glowing overhead.

"This is us," said Zimra, as she and Ulli muscled their way through the throng of termites clogging the doorway. Choosing the path with an "All You Can Eat!" billboard hanging over it, they wheeled the flies to a large dining room chock full of the most enticing array of food they had ever seen in one place. It was twice as much food as was available in the Diterra market, only not an ounce of it was rotten, rancid, or expired. The room was jampacked with termites filling their plates—sometimes two or three plates at a time—and each of the diners wore a little crown exactly like Queen Dalna's.

"Wow!" exclaimed Waverly and Oliver.

"This is nothing," said Zimra. "The Magical Musical Mystery Buffet will blow you away. It starts in a few hours so make sure you save some room. You're going to love it!"

Zimra and Ulli wheeled the chairs up to a table in the corner of the room. At the table next to them sat a bloated termite, happily eating alone. He looked like he was about to say something to them but didn't want to speak with a full mouth. Before he finished chewing, however, he filled his face with some other delicacy and never said a word.

Ulli said, "Wait here. We'll be back soon with some delicious food."

The sisters returned in less than a minute with two large plates overflowing with edible goodies—all sorts of berries, nuts, melons, and gourds waiting to be devoured. Old favorites, like apple, shared the plate with strange looking fruits they had never tasted or even seen before like pomegranates, kiwis, and lychees. It was piled so high they could barely see over the top to look at each other.

"No need to wait for us," directed Zimra. "Dig in."

"A'en't chu doe-in' to eat too?" asked Waverly.

"Not right now," Ulli said. "You see, we're workers, and workers aren't allowed to eat this food. We're really not supposed to eat when we're working either. Besides, this dining room is only for Kings and Queens. Queen Dalna would be very cross if she found us eating here."

"That's enough Ulli," chided Zimra. "Our guests should be able to enjoy their meal without having to listen to your complaining."

"They asked, so I answered," said Ulli.

"Go on, eat up," said Zimra ignoring her sister. "You need your strength. You poor things must be famished."

"Dut, it'd be wude to eat in pwont ob you," said Oliver.

Zimra sighed. Looking at her sister sternly, she said, "Now our guest is under the impression he would be rude to accept Queen Dalna's gracious hospitality. That's why we don't mention those things to guests, Ulli." Turning to Oliver, Zimra's voice turned sweet: "It's very considerate of you to want to share your food with us, but remember Queen Dalna generously gave it to you. It would be rude, not to mention foolish, to refuse it. Ulli was right about one thing though: this dining room is only for Kings and Queens. You have to have your coronation ceremony before you can eat here."

Oliver's and Waverly's eyes lit up when Zimra and Ulli each revealed the tiny crowns they had been hiding behind their backs. Then, with great pomp the sisters placed the coronets upon the flies' heads with utmost care. Zimra proclaimed, "You shall now be known as King Owiber, the Gallant, and you shall be Queen Waberwy, the Wise."

"What about Qeen Dawna?" asked Waverly. "Won't see be mad?"

"Why would Queen Dalna be mad?"

"Betause Dawna's Qeen," answered Oliver. "Dhe'e tan only be one Qeen."

"Not in this mound. There are thousands of Kings and Queens," said Zimra.

"And tens of thousands of workers who slave away so they never have to lift a fat, little finger," said Ulli, "unless it's to shove more food in their faces."

Zimra shot her sister a withering glance and said, "Enough, Ulli." Turning to the flies, she explained, "You come from the outside, where one ruler reigns over all. But inside this mound you are your own King and your own Queen. What Ulli was trying to say so unartfully is that we are working to make your stay as comfortable as possible. Remember, you're royals now. And what royals want, they shall have—too much is not enough. Now eat up. We'll be right back." Zimra took Ulli by the arm, giving her a hard squeeze as she led her out of the room.

Waverly and Oliver were embarrassed to have caused a rift between the sisters, but Zimra's words gave comfort. And soon the fragrant food was all they could think about. The flavor unleashed in the first bite was so wonderful, they quickly got over any lingering inhibitions.

They started with their old favorites, then ventured into the unfamiliar. Eagerly, they shared each fresh discovery with a "hewe, taste dis," or a "you habe to twy dis me-won." This meal, far surpassing any they had eaten in Diterra, was such a pleasant distraction they began to think differently about their troubles.

"Dis might tound t'azy," said Oliver, "but I want to 'tay hewe, in da mound."

"I was tinking da tame ting."

"Betta' to tay hewe as King, and be tomportable ..."

"... dan to die outtide por who knows what ..."

"... and who knows whewe," finished Oliver.

They were relieved to find they were of like mind. Their journey thus far had been difficult and dangerous, and the next day promised only to be more so. They knew they did not have much time left. Did they want to spend that time searching, possibly in vain, for something that might save them, or enjoy the time they had left indulging in every comfort to which they were entitled as newly minted royalty? A couple bites of this heavenly food proved to be irresistible persuasion.

Ulli and Zimra returned with two more heaping plates in their hands. "Dessert," said Zimra. The flies were quite full already but glad for another helping of succulent goodies. Waverly and Oliver informed the sisters of their decision to stay in the mound. Zimra gushed with approval. Ulli could barely force a smile.

CHAPTER FOURTEEN
WAKING UP

Hours passed, and the night slipped away. As the sun crept up over the horizon, Croda knelt once more before Ramsay's throne. Even though all the formalities of this ritual had been observed, something was different. Something was wrong, and the prophet trembled.

Normally Ramsay delighted at the fright he instilled in others, but sensing fear in his otherwise unflappable soothsayer was discomforting. Only a message bringing bad news could unsettle his prophet so thoroughly. "Tell me just as you have seen, and you will have my protection," said Ramsay, concerned fear would lead Croda to omit the unpleasant parts. "Yesterday you told me one who is blind will be the first to see the victor. By the way you're shaking, I take it today's message is not about victory."

"Perceptive, my master," replied Croda with a quavering voice. "Today's message is about loss."

The prophet paused to gather himself, but Ramsay bristled. "Tell me!" he thundered. "Don't leave me to guess!"

"Your messenger will serve the rebel," stammered the cricket. "And, if left unchecked, that messenger will damage your Kingdom, my Lord."

"What kind of damage? What will he do?"

"Grave damage, irreparable. Further word than this I have not received. I can only deliver the vision as I have seen it. Interpreting and understanding is reserved for you, my Lord."

"Understanding? It's obvious, isn't it? There's a traitor in our midst aiding my enemies."

"If it pleases my Lord, may I take my leave?"

"Fine," huffed Ramsay. After the prophet made his exit, Ramsay paced around his throne preoccupied with the thought of who might betray him. To calm himself, he climbed onto his web and sunk his teeth into a bug wrapped in a cocoon of spider silk. Ramsay slurped the bug's innards out of the white casing and into his belly in a matter of seconds. It did little to ease his worried mind.

***

While Waverly and Oliver binged in their regal dining room, Ben stirred from his unwelcome sleep. If not for a tiny crack under the door that allowed in only the faintest light, he would have been enveloped in total darkness. When he sat up his head throbbed, he found his left arm in a sling, and it hurt to move.

"Where am I?" he wondered, as he tried to replay the events leading up to their arrival at the mound. Gradually, the haze lifted from his mind. "Heading home, racing, talked about the

Queen, ran into spiders ... Spiders! The Hive! I've got to get them to the Hive!"

Ben sprang out of bed and ran to the door. "Oohh, how long have I been asleep?" He was panicked, fearful of the consequences if he had slept too long. "Oliver? Waverly? Are you in here?" He fumbled through the darkness until he found the door handle. It would not move; the door was locked. "You've got to be kidding me." Ben rammed his right shoulder into the door, trying to force it open, but it didn't budge. After a few more attempts, his shoulder was sore, and the door showed no sign of giving. He stepped back and kicked it a few times with no better luck.

"A key. Maybe there's a key somewhere," he said. By the soft glow sneaking in under the door, Ben fumbled around the room looking for a key or something he could use to knock the door down. Nothing. Other than the bed he had slept on, there was no furniture in the room and certainly no key.

Starting to the left of the door, he ran his hands along the wall looking for another door handle, a lever to a secret passage, anything to get him out of there. Again, he came up empty.

Standing next to the door with his head pressed against the wall, he tried to think of something, anything he could do to get out of that room. The harder he thought, the blanker his mind got.

"I don't have time for this! If I can't get out, then ... then ..." Ben shivered at the conclusion that thought invited. Shouting a furious "NO!", Ben pounded the wall with all his might. He half-expected to break his other arm but was so frustrated he did not care. But rather than clutching his fist in agony, he watched it sail clear through the wall, meeting with such little resistance it was as though he had done nothing more than punch the air. When he pulled his arm back, a dim light from the hallway poked through the hole he had made.

He hardly believed this spurt of good fortune. Impatient to find his friends—he only hoped he was not too late—Ben took a few steps back and ran as hard as he could into and through the wall. A second later, he was sprawled out on the hallway floor with a cloud of dust dancing and swirling around him in the diffuse light.

He could not help but admire the Ben-shaped hole he left in the wall as he brushed himself off. Ben barely remembered arriving at the mound before he passed out and guessed he must be somewhere inside of it. He only hoped he could find Waverly and Oliver.

Ben yanked open several nearby doors. Behind some were empty rooms, while others revealed surprised, sleepy termites. After disturbing a half dozen termites and noticing there were more doors on the hallway than he could count, Ben concluded searching this way would take more time than he could spare.

A memory suddenly flickered in his mind: a crowded room with elevators, stairs, and a trapeze. "That's where I last saw them," he muttered. Some termites emerged from behind one of the doors, and Ben followed them through a labyrinth of hallways until he ended up standing under a "Recovery Rooms Available" sign on a giant platform overlooking the great hall.

Ben found himself surrounded, the only fly in a sea of termites. "At least Waverly and Oliver should stick out," he said. He forced his way to the edge of the platform, turned to the crowd and yelled, "Anybody seen any flies?"

No one paid any attention to him. He climbed up on the railing, hoping more bugs would mind him if they could see him, and yelled again. A couple of termites looked his way this time, but none answered. They were all too focused on getting where they were going to take any time even to think about what Ben was asking.

Frustrated, Ben jumped into the crowd and pulled termites aside to ask them directly if they had seen any flies. At last, he found one who had; the sixteenth termite Ben asked pointed to the opposite side of the great hall toward some signs and mumbled, "over there."

Ben unhanded the termite, and gave his thanks over his shoulder as he ran up the stairs. He could not help but notice that only the skinny worker termites used the rickety stairs; the plump ones with crowns on their heads took the elevators. As he raced by one of the workers, Ben brushed against the chipped, flaking wall, causing a huge chunk of it to break loose. The debris smashed through the staircase and plummeted to the ground where it turned into a pile of dust on impact.

The staircase shook so violently Ben thought the whole thing was going to collapse. "Just because termites walk everywhere doesn't mean I have to." He beat his wings and took to the air.

He zipped over to the signs the termite had pointed out. While Ben was surprised to narrowly evade a collision with airborne trapeze artists in mid-stunt and in midair, he was not nearly as surprised as they were. Fortunately, there was a net below to break their fall, so Ben did not feel too bad for breaking their concentration.

When he reached the platform Ben saw a separate hallway under each of the signs. He could only wonder down which of the hallways the termite had seen Waverly and Oliver. Not wanting to pry answers out of termites again, he took off down the hall on the right.

At the far end of a dim corridor lined with old posters featuring performers of years gone by were two muscular termites standing watch in front of a door. A velvet rope hung across the threshold to prevent unauthorized entry. As Ben approached, the termites stood shoulder to shoulder in front of him and asked, "You got i.d.?"

"No," Ben answered. "Did you see two flies go in there?"

"Hey pal, we don't divulge information about our customers. But you look old enough—why don't you go in and look for yourself?" They pulled back the rope so Ben could go inside.

He entered a smoky room smothered in red light. Hundreds of termites crowded around a stage with nothing but a bare table and a single chair on it. Ben scanned the theater for Waverly and Oliver. Suddenly, an announcer's voice filled the room: "Are you ready, termites! Please give a warm welcome to Madame Detrivora!" The termites pushed closer to the stage and unleashed wild applause.

A well-fed termite with long fluttering eyelashes came out and waved to the adoring crowd. She took a seat at the table and tied a bib around her neck. When the applause died down, a termite dressed as a butler walked out on stage and served Madame Detrivora a plate loaded with three pieces of wood. "Oak, elm, and ash," announced the butler before walking off stage.

Madame Detrivora picked up the piece of elm and devoured the whole thing in less than five seconds, leaving only a cloud of saw dust hanging over the stage. The crowd went wild. Several termites passed out.

This is the weirdest thing I've ever seen, thought Ben.

Next she picked up the ash wood, which she downed in less than three seconds. When it seemed like the audience could not possibly get any more boisterous, she belched her satisfaction, and their roar became deafening.

It occurred to Ben that Waverly and Oliver would have no interest in this spectacle, so he bolted out the door, back to the platform. This time he ducked down the corridor on the left, which led him to a gigantic buffet.

He scoured the room, but found no flies. He felt someone here must have seen them so he went from table to table asking each diner if they had seen his friends. Many said no, while others concentrated so intently on their food they gave no response at all. Finally, a portly termite dining alone in the corner of the room nodded his head in response to Ben's questioning.

"You've seen them?" Ben double-checked. "Where did they go?"

The fat termite kept nodding and held up his hand as if to say, "Give me a moment to chew my food, then I'll tell you." Ben waited. The termite chewed and chewed and chewed while Ben paced in front of him. Eventually, he swallowed. Without saying a word, the termite reached for more food and would have shoveled it into his mouth had Ben not stopped him.

"Wait!" Ben scolded. "Weren't you going to tell me something?"

"Oh yeah. Nearly forgot," he said in a round, jolly voice. "There were two flies here—sat right next to me. Left maybe ten, fifteen minutes ago."

"Do you know where they were going?" asked Ben.

"They weren't going anywhere. Said they wanted to stay right here."

"But they're not here," said Ben, looking from side to side to help him make his point. "Are you sure that's what they said?"

"Not here, as in the dining room; here, as in the mound. And yes, I'm sure. They were sick; sat in wheel chairs to help them move and sounded unwell when they spoke. I wanted to know what was wrong with them in case they were contagious. I never did find out, but I understood them to say if they haven't long to live then they might as well be comfortable and enjoy the time they got left. So they decided to stay here—in the mound, that is."

"That's impossible. We're going to the Hive. They could be healed there."

"Heard it with my own ears: they planned on staying. And I don't blame them; can't imagine there is anything at the Hive that would make me want to give all this up."

"Ok, fine, they want to stay here," said Ben, "but where did they go?"

"Said they were going to the great hall to watch the circus acts while they waited for the Magical Musical Mystery Buffet to begin. That reminds me, I have to head down that way myself."

"Thanks for your help." Ben tore out of the dining room and back into the main hall. Without breaking his stride, he planted his foot on the platform railing and took a flying leap out into the cavernous great hall. The rail split in half under his weight.

He nose-dived toward the spectators watching the circus acts, hoping to spot Waverly and Oliver in the crowd. Ben was so focused on finding them, he failed to notice the group of termites swinging toward him on the trapeze. They, in contrast, noticed Ben and were horrified to see him again. One of the termites lost his grip and the whole group of them plunged into the net below, barely missing Ben as they fell.

He called out "sorry" and a split second later heard two familiar voices cry out, "Ben!"

He followed the sound down to Waverly and Oliver, who were sitting in their wheel chairs beside the bleachers. Shock swept over him at how much their physical appearance had changed since he saw them last. Their hands and arms were gnarled and they hunched over in their chairs. Their tongues had swollen so much they could not keep their mouths closed. Ben landed between them and hugged them both. "Am I ever glad to see you two! Thank goodness you're still alive."

Waverly gave him a crooked little smile. "Ben! You'we alwight!"

"We powgot about you," confessed Oliver.

"Well, I didn't forget you," said Ben with a smile. "Come on. We have to get out of here if we're going to make it to the Hive on time."

Ben reached for the handles of their wheel chairs, but Zimra held up her hand and said, "Hold on. I think they have something they want to tell you first. Don't you?"

Both Waverly and Oliver looked at the ground as Ben looked right at them. With her head down, Waverly said, "We tink we should tay he'e. We'we tomportable in da mound, and it's safe."

"But you'll die if you stay here," said Ben. "Where's the comfort or safety in that?"

"But wook at you," said Oliver. "It neaw'y tilled you just getting us dis par. We should just twy to enjoy the time we hab weft."

"There's no way I'm giving up on you, and you can't give up on me." Neither Waverly nor Oliver could bring themselves to look up at him.

"I'm actually glad you found us, Ben," said Ulli. "Waberwy and Owiber, you should listen to your friend. If you stay too long, you won't ever get out."

"That's enough!" scolded Zimra.

"Did I say something that wasn't true?"

"You might not like working for Queen Dalna, but you need to remember who your master is. You've been trying to spoil everything we've offered them since they got here. Just because you want to turn your back on Queen Dalna doesn't mean everyone else should."

"Yes, everyone should. And Queen Dalna would do well to turn her own back on this herself. Life should be more than amusing ourselves to death."

Zimra ignored Ulli and turned to Waverly and Oliver to plead, "Please ignore them. The Magical Musical Mystery Buffet is starting soon, and I would hate for them to ruin it for you."

"We don't have time for that," said Ben. "We have to go right now."

Just then, a loud buzzer sounded, leaving their ears ringing long after it stopped. Boisterous music wafted down from a termite band suspended from the ceiling high above the hall.

The sudden change in the termites' behavior was more startling than either of those things. Pure bedlam ensued as thousands of termites dropped whatever they had been doing to charge aimlessly around the hall, running every which direction and knocking each other over in their haste. Almost magically, two long buffet tables rose up out of the floor, one in the corner farthest from where the flies stood and the other very near to where they had been watching the circus. Instantly, every last termite zeroed in on one of the two tables, swarming all over each other desperately trying to get some food from the buffet.

"Behold!" announced Zimra, "The Magical Musical Mystery Buffet, the signature attraction of this mound. The buffet tables appear like magic. But the tables are above ground for less than a minute, then they disappear. Where will they spring up next? I don't know; it's a mystery. What do you say? Everybody loves it. Want to try it?"

"No! Don't try it," shouted Ulli over the din. "It's the same junk with more noise and distractions. You really should go with Ben."

"Ulli!" shouted Zimra. "That's it! I have had it with you creating problems. I'm telling Queen Dalna, and you're going to be in big trouble."

"See if I care! This is more important!"

"Fine, have it your way," said Zimra before marching off on a mission to find Dalna.

After she had taken ten steps, the buzzer sounded again. The tables the termites had been eating off of were swallowed up by the ground. The termites scattered and began rushing about in all directions again. A moment later another long buffet table popped up out of the floor only a few feet behind Zimra. The meandering termite mob became a crush rushing toward her, who was caught between them and their food. She tried to get out of their way, but there were too many of them coming at her too quickly. First she was bumped, then shoved, and then knocked to the ground. Zimra cried out for help as she was being stomped on.

"Zimra!" Ulli started toward her sister but could not fight her way through the crowd. None of the other termites noticed either of them and pressed ahead for their turn at the buffet table.

"I'll get her!" hollered Ben. He shot up high over the throng and, after spotting Zimra, launched himself like a missile into the termites, ramming a few with his shoulder. His broken arm throbbed, but he managed to knock them clear of Zimra for a second. As he scooped her up, he was bumped, pushed, and nearly knocked over. Zimra clung tightly to Ben as he tried to fly, but the termites were so close against him he lacked the space he needed to beat his wings. Ben planted his hand on a termite's shoulder and leapt, vaulting himself into the air. He made it high enough that he could flap his wings and get some lift. As Ben rounded back toward Ulli and the flies, Zimra caught an aerial view of the termites crawling all over each other.

When they landed, Ulli threw her arms around her sister and asked, "Are you all right?"

"Not really," answered Zimra. "They would have trampled me to death. For what? A fistful of fruit tart? And this by bugs I've served faithfully. But a fly I don't even know, who has every right to be mad at me, risks his life to save mine. I'm asking them to give that up? Why? So they can get trampled too?"

"Sis," started Ulli, but Zimra quickly cut her off.

"You've been right all along. You've been telling me, and I kept telling you how ridiculous you were being. You were right, Ulli. You are so right—we have to help them get out of here."

Zimra was not the only one moved by Ben's heroics. Waverly and Oliver now looked right at their friend. "We'we sowwy, Ben. It just seemed so much easi-ah to tay hewe."

"It is," answered Ben, "but it's not worth it."

139

"I'm gwad you tame back for us," said Waverly.

"Me too," said Ben. "Now we have to get out of here."

Zimra and Ulli led the flies back to the wall where they originally entered the mound, but the hole had been patched up. "Looks like we'll have to get them out," said Ulli. She set her powerful jaws to work gnawing a way out for them.

Zimra stopped her after a few bites. "I have a better idea. Remember when we worked the Magical Musical Mystery Buffet? What was the one thing they told us never to do?"

"Never raise two tables right next to each other," answered Ulli.

"Why did they tell us that?" asked Zimra.

"I never really knew."

"Because," Zimra explained, "they didn't think the mound could withstand the force if everyone rushed in the same direction at the same time."

"What does that have to do with anything?"

"Do you remember," replied Zimra coyly, "where they keep the backup controls for the Mystery Buffet?"

"Of course, but ..." Ulli's face lit up once she finally understood what her sister had in mind. "You are absolutely brilliant!"

"Let's do it then," said Zimra. "Ben, you stay here, right against this wall. Cover their heads, and no matter how loud it gets, stay right where you are. You'll be out of here soon."

"Got it," said Ben.

"And I might not ever see you again," said Zimra as she gave him a big hug, "so thank you for saving me." Ulli and Zimra said tender farewells to Waverly and Oliver before disappearing around the corner. Ben positioned their wheel chairs against the wall, climbed between them, and pulled their heads into his chest.

They watched and waited. The band hanging from the ceiling continued to blare. The roar of the crowd came closer only to retreat to the other side of the room when the buzzer sounded again.

Without warning, the pace changed drastically. The buzzer sounded several times in rapid succession. Each time, a table shot up from the ground only to disappear before any termites could reach it. They grew confused and frustrated, running wildly, bumping into one another and knocking each other over. The band picked up their tempo with every change in buffet location. Their fast-paced music only made the scene more frantic.

When it seemed the termites' descent into utter chaos was complete, a louder, longer buzzer sounded as if emphatically declaring itself the final whistle. Ben saw two buffet tables spring up from the ground right next to each other on the opposite side of the hall. The termites regained their composure and within seconds were all rushing to the tables. The first ones there pounced on the food. When the second wave arrived, they pushed the first group off the table and against the wall. The latecomers then mashed the second bunch into and on top of the first.

Ben heard a barely audible creaking noise that seemed to emanate from the mound itself. Debris fell from the ceiling, turning into piles of dust when it hit the ground a few feet from where they stood. The creaking noise turned into a cracking sound, as a fault line spread along the wall just an inch or two above the floor. The ground beneath their feet rumbled as a thread of light slipped through the fissure and the mound trembled violently. Then a bright light poured through the crack as the wall rose higher and higher away from its foundation until gravity took it away. The mound was tipping over.

It came down with a loud crash then rolled away down a slight hill, taking the chaos and noise with it. As it disappeared from sight, a powerful silence took its place. Ben clung so tightly to Waverly and Oliver, they could barely breath. Dust swirled around them, coating them as it settled. He waited for any new noises, but when none came he slowly lifted his head and released his grip on his friends. To his great relief, Ben saw the sun peaking through the haze. He could tell it was before noon; they still had time.

As the air cleared, they saw their cart parked exactly where they had left it next to the mound. Floyd sat on the cart, yawning as though he had been aroused from a deep sleep. "What took you so long, Beesley?" he said. "I was starting to think I might never see you guys again."

CHAPTER FIFTEEN
DRIFTING

The mound's collapse left Ben dumbstruck. He scarcely believed two little termites could be capable of obliterating such an enormous structure in a matter of seconds. Floyd, in stark contrast, did not seem remotely surprised but was clearly impressed by the mass destruction he just witnessed.

"Kudos, Benny my boy, kudos. Believe me, I've got a lot of practice messing things up, but I don't think I could have pulled that off no matter how hard I tried. You simply have to tell me how you did it."

"What are you doing here?" asked Ben, who was equally stunned to find Floyd waiting for them.

"When did I last see you?" Floyd asked himself. "Oh, yeah, on the mountain. Well, after I left you guys I ran some errands. I happened to pass near here and saw a couple of punk ladybugs taking your cart for a joyride. I say to myself, 'That cart looks familiar.' Of course, I think of you. Then I noticed someone built these two little seats—not the most comfortable seats in the world, by the way—and I thought maybe you made these for your little buddies since they're not the steadiest on their feet.

"Anyway, the cart's not too far from this mound, so I figure you've taken my advice, you're inside with the termites, and it's up to me to stop them. So I say to the punks, 'That's not your cart. Put it back where you got it.' And they say, 'You gonna make us?' So I say, 'Have it your way,' and then I stick one of them and have a little snack. They run away crying and screaming, and I brought the cart back here. I've been sitting on it ever since to make sure nobody else tries to swipe it. But my belly's full, it's dark out—of course I fall asleep. Next thing I know, the mound is falling over, and you're here."

Even though Ben doubted the truthfulness of Floyd's story, he nevertheless felt strangely grateful. "Thanks for the help, Floyd," said Ben. "Now if you'll excuse me, you're in their seats."

"Still pressing on to the Hive, are we?" asked Floyd as he stepped off the cart.

"Yep," said Ben brusquely. He lifted Waverly and Oliver from their wheelchairs onto the cart. "We have to get there before sunrise tomorrow."

Ben took the cart by the handles and pushed it along the path that led to the big lake they had seen from the top of the mountain the night before. Off in the distance, far across the water, Ben could make out the faint image of the Hive nestled in the side of a mountain that towered over the horizon. For the first time, he saw his final destination with his own eyes. While it was still a long way off, simply having it in view filled him with hope that he would make it in time.

Floyd flew backwards alongside Ben. "So, I gotta know. You stop in for a bite to eat and a little rest. Knowing the termites, they invite you to stay. You say, 'we really must get going—oh, and sorry I knocked your place over?' I thought you all would have been very comfortable there. What gives?"

Ben recounted the events of the preceding night as best he could. While Ben was talking, Oliver rested his head on Waverly's shoulder. She lowered her head to rest against his. Only two siblings who had spent their whole lives together could so effortlessly find comfort in each other. With very little sleep over the last three days and not a wink during the night that just passed, they nodded off before Ben finished telling Floyd about coming down the mountain.

Other than an occasional interruption when he felt the irresistible need to poke fun, tell Ben what he did wrong, or generally be obnoxious, Floyd mostly kept his mouth shut and barely seemed himself. Ben was glad to have someone to talk to, and Floyd appeared surprisingly interested in listening for once.

By the time Ben finished telling his tale, they had reached the lake's shore. The lake was wide and murky, filled deep with rusty brown water. A cool, steady wind rippled across its surface. The path they had been walking disappeared at the water's edge. Ben looked to the left and right, but saw no path and no bridges, only water. "Where did it go?" uttered Ben in disbelief. "Where do we pick up the path?"

"There is no more path," Floyd replied. "It stops at the lake."

"But how will we get around the lake?"

"Oh," said Floyd, "that might be a problem. The lake is really, really wide and surrounded by mountains on either end. To go around it, you would have to walk the length of the lake, pass over a mountain, and that would put you back on a path to the Hive. Straight on from there should take you a day or two."

"You know, we came this way in the first place because you said it would take a day or two," Ben reminded him.

"Doesn't sound like something I'd say," said Floyd.

"You just said it three seconds ago! And you told us the same thing yesterday; it's the only reason we came this way!"

"Gee, I'm sorry. Guess I'm not really that great with estimates. I thought you would have been a lot closer to the Hive by now. How could I have known it would take you this long?"

"It's taken so long because you sent us through a jungle where we got kidnapped and nearly killed by a psychopathic ant."

"To be fair," argued Floyd, "you probably spent more time overnighting with the termites than you did going through the jungle or coming down the mountain."

"We only stayed with the termites because I got knocked out taking the short cut you suggested. And they nearly didn't let us leave even though you told us we should stay with them. It's like you're trying to sabotage us."

"Whoa, whoa, whoa. Clearly that's not the case, or I wouldn't have saved your cart from those ladybugs. I could have just let them have it, and you'd be stuck. Instead I stuck my neck out to help you guys, and this is how you thank me."

"I don't have any proof you actually did that, do I? I would have to take you at your word, which would be pretty stupid of me."

"Fine. I help you; you insult me."

"Don't pretend to be innocent, Floyd."

"I thought you were in a big hurry to get somewhere. Seems like you're the one wasting time now."

Floyd was right. Ben felt silly having gotten so sidetracked. Floyd was a problem, but Ben did not have time to dwell on him. He needed to figure out how to get Waverly and Oliver to the other side of the lake. Staring out over the water, the thought of attempting to cross it made Ben queasy. He scanned the shoreline hoping for an easier way.

"Forget it," said Floyd softly. "I know you think I'm a liar, but I'm telling you honestly, going over the lake is your only option. Every other way will take too long."

Ben didn't say anything. He looked back at the lake and felt like throwing up. Flies are not made for water. They lack the special adaptations needed to thrive around lakes. Flies get bogged down if they get wet. Their wings stick together so they can't fly. Beads of water get trapped between the hairs on their bodies, making it difficult for them to breathe. Just the thought of getting near so much water was disorienting and intimidating to a fly.

Sensing Ben's anxiety over the prospect of an attempted lake crossing, Floyd said, "You don't have to do it, you know. They're lost anyway. Why throw your life away too?"

"Be quiet!" Ben yelled. In an instant, his queasiness morphed into determination. He pulled Waverly and Oliver from the cart and gently laid them on the coarse sand a few feet from the shore. Through it all they never stirred from their sleep. Ben waded into the lake, pulling the cart behind him until the water reached his waist. To his relief, the cart floated. He shook it with all his strength, but it stayed steady, showing no sign of tipping. He hopped aboard, and it easily held his weight.

Ben seemed pleased with his experimenting and dragged the cart back to shore. Waverly and Oliver were so exhausted they still didn't stir when Ben hoisted them back into their seats. After confirming they were still breathing, Ben shoved off. He ran alongside them until the water reached his waist then jumped onto the back of their makeshift boat.

As they drifted away from land, Ben sunk with dread at the prospect of being stuck in the middle of a lake. He sought comfort in the thought that every second on the water put him a second closer to the opposite shore, but even this small consolation was tarnished when Floyd landed on the front of the cart asking, "Mind if I join you?"

Just then, Oliver turned his head from side to side and kicked his feet as he muttered, "No. No. No." Although Oliver was in the throes of a dream, Ben let his answer stand for them both.

"I know it looks bad," said Floyd, "and a lot of times I come off as a big jerk, but I really just wanted to help. Besides, you shouldn't be alone out here."

"I wouldn't be alone," said Ben as he double-checked that Waverly's and Oliver's seat belts were fastened. Floyd ignored Ben and sat quietly on the front of the boat. Ben did not protest. The next hour passed in silence except for the noise of water gently lapping against their cart. There was a light breeze, and the sun stayed hidden behind the haze.

Before setting out that day, Ben knew nothing about boating. This fact explains why he had no sails and no paddle, which in turn explains why they bobbed in the water, barely moving toward the opposite shore in that first hour. Having made such little progress, Ben panicked when the direction of the wind changed, and he found himself drifting backwards. It became clear he would have to take a more active role in getting them to the other side.

After a thorough review of items on hand, Ben concluded the handles, if removed from the cart, could be used for navigational purposes. Leaning over the back end of the boat, he hurriedly tried to untie the rope holding the handles in place. But there were so many knots, each tied very tightly. "Who tied these?" he wondered as he struggled to free the stick.

Ben was hanging over the back working on a knot when he heard a splash from near the front. He popped up to see what had made the noise. Oliver was in his chair, but Waverly's was empty. Ben jumped to his feet and looked over the chair and into the water. There was Waverly, thrashing, desperately trying to stay afloat.

Ben darted after her. Skimming the surface of the water, he reached for her hands but was too late. She had dipped under and was slowly sinking. Oliver helplessly watched in jaw-dropped horror.

Ben sped back to the boat and grabbed the vine that was tied to the cart—the very one that had dragged him down the mountain. With the vine clutched firmly in hand, he shot into the lake.

The second he entered, he felt the water close around him, squeezing him as if trying to force the air from his body. Fortunately, the momentum from his dive carried him most of the way to Waverly. If he could reach out quickly he could grab her hand, but his arms moved through the water like they were stuck in slow motion. By the time he extended his hand, he had missed her by a centimeter. He pumped his legs to get closer, but the vine was extended as far as it would go. On the surface, Ben had pulled the boat directly overhead and made it tip so severely every time he kicked that Floyd nearly fell in too. Waverly looked up to see Ben reaching for her and, unable to coordinate her muscle movement any more, did the only thing she could: flail. Her flailing arm landed right in Ben's open hand.

He drew her close, held her tightly, turned to the surface, and pulled himself up the vine with his other hands. The water felt thick, more like he was crawling through mud than swimming in a lake. After taking each fistful of vine, he wondered where he would get the strength to take another, but each time he did, it got a little brighter as they got closer to the surface.

At last he broke out of the water and gasped deeply for air. Even though that one breath was not enough to fill his lungs, he still felt guilty for inhaling before Waverly's head was above water. When he did manage to pull her out, she came up choking.

Placing his foot on the side of the cart for support, Ben struggled, but finally lifted her out of the lake onto her seat. As she lay on her side, her head resting on Oliver's lap, she expelled the water that she had swallowed. Then she rolled to her back, her chest heaving rapidly as she tried to breathe. Ben pulled himself onto the cart, still struggling to return his breathing to normal. He leaned over Waverly's seat, put his hand on her shoulder, and told her between gasps that she was safe now.

Ben saw one half of Waverly's lap belt in Oliver's hand. He looked to the other side to find the other half dangling in the water. *How could her belt have come undone*, he wondered. *Surely, she couldn't undo it herself* .... "Floyd," growled Ben, "what did you do?"

"You know," said Floyd calmly from the front of the boat, "this reminds me of a joke. See, this bug says 'waiter there's a fly in my soup.' And the waiter says ..."

"This isn't a joke Floyd. What did you do?"

"It's for your own good," Floyd yelled back at Ben. "You're going to throw your life away helping them. And for what? Nothing!"

"They're not nothing! They're everything to me; I have to save them!"

"Do you really think Ramsay is going to help you? Do you think he's going to be so moved by how much you love your little buddies that he'll let them live?"

Ben said nothing.

"Oh my gosh, that's it, isn't it? That's your plan? That's all you got? Fly boy, either you're delusional or just plain stupid. Ramsay is not going to help you, I promise."

"Once he realizes how far I'll go to save them, he'll have no choice but to set them free."

"The only way to set them free is to take Ramsay off the throne. I wondered once if that was what you came here to do, to lead a rebellion. Boy, was I wrong. Look at you. No followers. Cut, bruised, a broken arm, and black eyes—you're hanging on by a thread, and you haven't even made it to the Hive yet. But you think Ramsay's wittle heart is going to break and he'll give you what you want."

"We'll see."

"Nobody cares for them but you."

"They matter to the Queen, Floyd. And so do you."

"Oh, not that Queen nonsense. If she cared about any of us or was strong enough to beat Ramsay, she'd be here already. But she's not. You know why? The Queen is dead. She's dead, and you're following her to the grave. All for them. If I were you, I would push 'em in, let 'em sink to the bottom and set *yourself* free.

No one, and I mean no one, would blame you. Not me. Not Ramsay. And certainly not any Queen."

With a menacing look in his eyes, Floyd took a step toward Waverly and Oliver. Before he could take another, Ben met him head-on with a flying tackle. They tumbled end over end until they came to a stop on the bow of the boat. Floyd was laid out flat on his back, the crown of his head dipped in the water. Ben sat on top of him, pinning his shoulders to the boat.

"I've been able to live with your lies until now Floyd, but they've gotten too dangerous. If you ever try to hurt them again, you'll have me to deal with. And I won't be nearly as forgiving as I am now."

Floyd squirmed uncomfortably. "Owwww! You cut me!"

"You're making it up," said Ben.

"I'm serious. Look." Floyd wriggled his hand free and slipped it down to his belly. He pulled back a bloodied palm and held it up for Ben to see.

"I ... I don't know how that happened," said Ben, "but I'm going to let you up. When I do, you are to leave this boat at once. Understand?"

Ben let go of Floyd, and the mosquito flew off as instructed, pausing only to call Ben a few names and complain about the scratch running down his gut. Soon he had floated out of earshot, and the three flies were all alone, drifting on the lonely lake. As Ben stood up, he noticed a smear of blood on his tail. *That's odd,* he thought, *how could I have cut him?*

CHAPTER SIXTEEN
PRISONERS OF THE LAKE

Only when Floyd had flown far enough away did Ben feel comfortable turning his back on him to help Waverly sit up in her seat. Ben tenderly pushed her antennae out of her face. Despite the fear that had gripped her so tightly only moments before, she giggled softly and smiled; her swollen tongue poked out of her mouth. She took his hand and held it. Ben was glad to see her comforted after her horrifying underwater ordeal.

Suddenly, Ben screamed, "Owww!" and yanked his hand free. Waverly had bitten him. "Why did you do that?" he asked.

Waverly leaned close to his face and loudly said, "Daddy at werk! Daddy, daddy, daddy werk!" She kicked her legs wildly and bounced out of her seat with such energy she would have fallen back into the lake if Ben had not buckled her in. Just as quickly as she started, she was done and now stared quietly across the water, chewing on her own hand.

A thought, sad and persistent, overwhelmed Ben: Waverly did not smile and laugh because she had been soothed. She bit his hand because the part of her mind that told her what she should and should not bite had been overrun by spider venom; she no longer knew any better. Likewise, she had no idea what she was saying. It was exactly as Noth had predicted.

After Ben pulled Waverly's hand from her mouth, he tapped Oliver on the leg and asked, "You okay?"

Oliver raised his hands over his head and pulled on his antennae. Tipping his head back, he giggled a little bit before calling out, "D-I'm bein' dood. Moooo." He let out his own brand of manic, happy-sounding laughter as he patted his belly.

Their laughing was grossly out of place next to the sadness that consumed Ben. He knew he was losing them; this was just another in a long line of painful reminders. How he wished he could remember the last thing they had said to him when their words had meaning. As hard as he tried, Ben could not recall those words.

When Ben raised his head, tears welling in his eyes, he realized they had drifted back to the side of the lake they had started from. *No time to wallow,* he thought, *I have to get us moving.* He gave Waverly and Oliver a kiss on the head, then crawled over them to the back of the boat to work on loosening that knot again. After another minute of tugging and untangling, Ben had the rope untied and held the stick in his hands.

First, he lowered the pole into the water to push off against the bottom of the lake, but the stick was too short to reach. Next, he tried using it as an oar, but it was too thin to propel them through the water. Nothing he tried worked. When it became apparent his efforts with the stick were futile, Ben screamed in frustration and flung it far across the murky water.

He plopped down on the back of the boat and dangled his feet in the water. The sun had already crested and was on its way down. Sitting with his elbows on his legs, palms pressed against his cheeks, he heard, "daddy, daddy werk," followed by some hearty laughter. *At least Waverly and Oliver enjoy being on the lake,* thought Ben. The fact they no longer understood the danger they were in made Ben feel even more responsible for them and increasingly on his own. As Floyd so callously reminded him: nobody was going to save them but him.

While he sat, Ben kicked his feet. He noticed each kick sent a ripple through the water and that each subsequent kick put him further away from the first ripple, so Ben started kicking furiously. The boat was moving, but slowly. Propping himself up on the back of the boat, he sunk his legs further into the water and kept kicking. While this was more effective—the boat was moving more quickly—he could not hold that position much longer.

There has to be another way, he thought. He raced through other options in his mind. It suddenly hit him, and he gulped. *Anything but that.* The queasy feeling he thought he had left on shore came roaring back with the strength of a tornado. The best option, Ben reluctantly concluded, was for him to slip into the water, hold onto the back of the boat, and kick as hard as he could. Glancing up at the descending sun, he was reminded there was not enough daylight left to dawdle. The time for thinking—and dreading—was over.

By the look on Ben's face, one would have thought he slipped into a barrel of snakes rather than a lake. The water was so cold it chased the air from his body. His chest tightened, but breaths still came and went as long as he kept his head above water.

Gripping the boat tightly, Ben laid himself out straight and started kicking.

He kicked and kicked and kicked with all his strength—what was left of it at least. All his effort rapidly drained him of energy, but he pushed on, every now and again looking up to make sure he was still headed in the right direction. He was obviously making progress and that happy fact was enough to keep him going.

After three hours of talking himself into taking just one more kick, Ben had made it over half way across but simply could not raise his foot one more time without a rest. He barely had enough strength left to pull himself back onto the boat, but he managed. Once he was out of the water, brutal cold racked his body—an unforgiving reminder that both winter and nightfall drew closer by the minute.

As Ben lay panting on the back of the boat, he heard Waverly sing, "To-my-o, da sun wi' tome out, to-my-o." He was glad to hear her voice, but it made him shiver even worse; the morning sun was the last thing he wanted to see.

When Waverly came to the end of her song, Oliver clapped his hands and let out a loud "Mmmoooooo!" as if it was his way of saying, "Bravo."

Ben looked back at the fading sun. *Less than an hour of daylight left and I'm still stuck on this lake.* For the first time Ben thought seriously about the consequences of failing to deliver them to the Hive on time. He felt all alone and wondered if Floyd was right—either the Queen was too weak to help, or maybe she just did not care. "I don't know where you are," he whispered through his doubt, "but I could really use some help."

His words still hung in the air when he spotted two red leaves drifting across the water drawing nearer to the boat. Even through the haze, the retreating sun made the lake sparkle and the leaves look like they were glowing. Ben kept his eyes on the leaves, wishing he could move as quickly and effortlessly as they did. Any envy he felt evaporated when they passed by the back of the cart, where Ben could see the leaves moved in perfect unison because a spider web had been strung between them. "Help me!" cried a beautiful black and orange-streaked butterfly who was stuck in the web. She was submerged underwater and had to raise her head above the surface to call out. "Oh, please save me!"

Ben jumped onto the remaining handle and reached out to grab her, but his hand only brushed through the water. She had passed just out of his reach and was drifting away quickly.

Ben very nearly slipped off the handle into the water. As he stabilized himself, he heard a second voice. "Please help me," it moaned. "I can't take any more." Ben looked to the other side of the boat and saw a dragonfly whose feet were stuck to a spider web floating between a peach pit and a twig. The dragonfly also kept sinking beneath the surface between his cries.

Ben looked back and forth between the butterfly and the dragonfly trying to figure out which one he should try to save first. He decided he must try to save the dragonfly before he too passed beyond his reach. Ben dove to the other side of the boat, landing behind Oliver's seat with his hand outstretched to grab hold of the dragonfly. Again, he missed by what seemed like a millisecond. "I'm sorry," Ben called. "I thought I had you."

With the dragonfly floating beyond his grasp, Ben spun around to check on the butterfly. To his surprise, she had boomeranged and was headed back toward the boat. Even more shocking was the sight of hundreds, and then thousands of leaves, sticks, nuts, and other pieces of flotsam, bobbing up and down on the lake following behind the butterfly. Between each piece of floating debris was another spider's web. There was at least one bug—whether beetles, gnats, moths, locusts, grasshoppers, fleas, termites, ants, or even flies—stuck on every web. And each one desperately begged for help. "Save us! Please do something! Don't leave me here alone!" Their cries were as loud as they were heartbreaking.

Ben watched the bugs getting closer when he suddenly felt the cart shake underneath his feet. A log had rammed against them from the other side. Ben leaned over to take hold of a gnat stuck on the web that was anchored to the log, but his hand passed right through the gnat and into the water. The gnat vanished from view for a moment until the water settled, and the gnat reappeared, fully formed and looking every bit as real as the boat underneath Ben's feet. "What on earth?" marveled Ben.

Before Ben could take in what had just happened, the boat shook again and again in rapid succession. All the floating objects were crashing into the boat and Ben struggled to keep his balance. He stumbled several times before falling behind Waverly and Oliver, his face stopping only inches from the water. In front of him, stuck to a web and staring back at him, was a red-eyed fly who made Ben think he might have been looking into a mirror.

"Save me, Ben," said the fly in the water.

Hearing his name rise off the lips of the doomed made him pause. "How do you know my name?" Rather than wait for an answer, Ben thrust his arm into the water to scoop up the fly. Just as with the gnat, Ben's arms passed clear through the fly as if he were only a mirage. This time though, when the water settled, and the bug reformed before him, Ben was staring into the face of a bee.

He jumped back in utter shock, refusing to fully trust his eyes. "You're a bee!" Ben said. "What are you doing here?"

"There's no where else I can go," answered the bee.

"But Ramsay killed all the bees."

"All but one. But I'm not the one who got away; I was the first to go."

Ben's face contorted with consternation. "Gron?"

"What's left of me."

"But he killed you; how can you still here?"

"This is where all who have perished under Ramsay's rule have ended up, eternally trapped beneath this lake."

"Well, you're above water now. There's got to be a way to get you out." Ben scanned the lake from end to end. In every direction, as far as he could see, insects stuck in webs pressed against each other, struggling to get closer to the boat.

"The only way to save us is to break the curse of Ramsay," replied Gron. "As long as his curse is upon us, we can never get back to the Queen. Our only hope is if the Queen comes for us, but she won't come until the curse is lifted."

"How will that happen?" asked Ben.

"How is less important than who will make it happen."

"Well, who then? Who can lift the curse?"

"You," stated Gron.

"Me? I can't even get across this lake."

"That's why we're here: to help you."

"Help me?" wondered Ben, as he noticed for the first time the strong wind that had blown his antennae into his eyes. He realized the hordes of lost bugs surrounding him were not only seeking help, but lending it as well by pushing the cart across the lake. Ben turned to see the shore he had longed to set foot on all day was only minutes away. He spun back around to Gron, "I thought I came here to save my friends; I can't be responsible for all of you too. There's too many of you."

"You worry you can't save them, yet you press on any way. Why would someone take on a lost cause with such dedication? Why not just give up?"

"Because I can't quit," answered Ben. "They need me, and I'll do whatever I need to for them."

"That's love. And love like yours is the only thing that will break the curse. If you save them, then you'll save us too."

Without warning the boat lurched to a stop. Ben fell backwards between Waverly and Oliver and rolled off the front of the boat onto dry land. He hopped up and flew over the water to thank Gron, but Gron and the other bugs were being hastily pulled back toward the center of the lake.

"What if I can't do this alone, Gron?" Ben called after him. "What if I need more help?"

"Look for the Keepers of the Light—they're expecting you. They've been waiting ages to prepare the way for the Queen's return."

"But you still haven't told me how."

"You will know how when the time comes. In fact, it will be the only thing that you can do if you follow where your love leads you." Gron started to say something else, but could no longer keep his head above water. Once Gron was submerged, Ben tuned in to the haunting wails and moans of the other insects: "Save me. Please saaaave me!"

As the bugs and their cries were pulled back into the lake by an unseen force, two web-stuck flies pushed their way up to Ben.

"Do you have our babies?" asked the female fly, fighting to keep her head up.

"Waverly," said the male, pausing only because his face dipped under the water. "And Oliver?"

Ben said, "I do, but, oh my, does that mean you're ..."

"Their parents ... yes," said their Dad.

"Please, Ben," said their Mom as she was being pulled away, "Save our babies! Please save them!"

"I'm doing everything I can," said Ben in a whisper. Then their cries for help were drowned out and once more there was no noise but the sound of the waves lapping against the boat. Ben, still shocked, turned and gazed up at the Hive. The soft moonlight outlined its contours against the darkness, making it look beautiful. The thought of what awaited him there, however, made him shudder.

CHAPTER SEVENTEEN
KEEPERS OF THE LIGHT

Ben struggled to extract the cart from the lake, but his task became more manageable as the water seeped out of it. When it had drained completely, gobs of lake gunk were left clinging to its sides. Various water plants had wrapped around the axles and splash-slapped the ground with every turn of the wheels.

Safely on land again, Ben checked on Waverly and Oliver as the cart dripped dry. Their eyes were open, but they did not answer his questions. Their faces looked swollen, and they shivered in the cold. They were alive, but the poison was taking its toll, wearing them down. For the first time Ben sensed they were in pain. No longer could he take comfort in the belief they were spared from hurting in spite of their afflictions.

Ben sought a path to follow but found only a grassy field spreading out in front of him. Across the field sat a thick grove of trees and towering beyond that was the Hive. It loomed over the garden against the night sky, looking foreboding and haunted. Still,

Ben knew he had to get there. Between his broken arm, the cart's missing handle, and the uneven ground, he labored to cross the field. He had not gone far when two thin black bugs with maroon wings folded over their backs approached them. They were fireflies.

"What are you doing out here?" asked one of the bugs. "Can't you see it's past curfew?"

"Curfew?" asked Ben. "What are you talking about?"

"Come on, everyone knows what curfew is," chided the bug, whose demeanor changed when he finally took a careful look at Ben. "Hold on—you're no firefly."

"You're right, I'm just a fly," said Ben. "Do you know where I could find the Keepers of the Light?"

The fireflies were taken aback by Ben's directness. "Who told you about them?"

"Some bugs I met near the lake," Ben replied, uncertain of how much he should tell them.

"Where are you going, and why do you want to know?" No one would mistake their questioning as friendly.

Waverly, rousing from her stupor, suddenly shouted, "Boo-boos huwt."

"What's this?" asked the firefly, inspecting the vines used to hold Waverly and Oliver in their seats.

"Oh, they're my friends. I'm trying to help them."

"Is that why they're tied up? Doesn't look like you're helping anybody."

"I can see how this might look bad, but I am trying to save them. I was hoping the Keepers of the Light would be able to help me get to them to the Hive."

"The Hive!" cried one of the fireflies in horror. "Who in their right mind would want to go there?"

"I know it sounds crazy, but the only way I can help them is to get them to the Hive. We need to see Ramsay."

The first firefly whispered to the other, "This guy is pretty weird. We'd better take him to the elders."

"Definitely," answered the second firefly. Turning to Ben, he said, "You need to come with us. Our elders will want to talk with you."

Ben was thrilled to feel, at last, like he was getting some help. He pushed the cart alongside the fireflies who flew on either side of him as they crossed the meadow. Having come through his isolation on the lake, Ben's spirits had been raised immeasurably. If even a fraction of the Queen's kindness and wisdom lived on in these fireflies, then he was sure to get Waverly and Oliver to the Hive in time. The thought was enough to put a real smile on his face, even if he had to wrestle with the cart just to keep it moving.

After a short walk, they came upon a gathering of half a dozen darkened fireflies sitting on stones in a half circle. The elders looked like they had been waiting for Ben. They sat in motionless silence and wore hoods that cast long shadows over their faces. His escorts made him wait as they approached the council and whispered in the ear of the Chief Elder who sat in the center. Then the guards took a place on either side of the elders, facing Ben.

The Chief Elder rose and cleared his throat. "In the name of our beloved, immortal Queen," he stated in a dignified manner, "who once ruled and who shall rule again, on behalf of the elders of the Keepers of the Light, I welcome you brother Ben."

The strange formality intrigued Ben. He had never spoken like that, but on this occasion felt like he should at least try. "Nice to meet you, also in the name of the Queen. I am the keeper of Waverly and Oliver, who are here on this humble cart."

"Dearest Ben," said the Elder, "please tell us why you have come to our meadow at such a strange hour."

Ben explained everything as quickly and plainly as he could, and concluded by saying, "I am only passing through on my way to Ramsay's Hive, where I hope my friends will be saved."

"My child, you cannot get to the Hive from here. As you should know, we have been chosen by the Queen to prepare the way for her return. To keep Ramsay from prying into our affairs, years ago we planted that grove of aspen trees. With our special gardening techniques, we grew the trees so big they joined together and are now impassable. No spider or bug, not even the smallest, could get through that forest. The trees keep Ramsay out, but it also keeps us in. But if we had not planted the aspens, we could not live as freely as we do."

Ben felt like he had been punched in the stomach when he heard this news. "Surely, there has to be some way around the aspen trees. There has to be some way to get to the Hive from here."

"There is one way, but I'm afraid I cannot divulge it. It's only for the elders to know."

"Please, sir, there has to be some way you can help us. If not for me, think of them. If I don't make it in time, they'll die."

"Well, Ben," said the Elder with a chilly stare, "as much as we would love to help you and your friends, under the circumstances, you have made it impossible for us to do anything. You see, you have broken some very, very important rules. And there must be consequences for rule-breaking. We would do you no favors if we spared you even the painful consequences of your disregard for the law. In the end, it's what's best for you."

"Rule-breaking?" said Ben in disbelief. "Would you mind telling me what rules we've broken?"

"With pleasure," the smirking Elder replied. "You violated curfew, which has been clearly posted throughout the meadow. You are traveling in mixed company, which is bad enough, but doing so after dark is an even worse offense. And your one-handled work vehicle isn't up to specifications, not to mention the fact it's improperly loaded."

"My work vehicle is improperly loaded?"

"That's right. It's for your safety and ours. And another thing: we don't appreciate your tone. One must give deference to his elders."

"My tone?"

"There it is again." The Elder stood as if to assert his authority. "You must mind your place and remember that to question the elders is to question the Queen herself. It was flippant, insolent, rule-breaking bugs like you who drove the Queen away in the first place." He got angrier with every word he uttered.

Ben's smile had been browbeaten from his face, and his renewed hope obliterated. He debated himself on whether Gron had been mistaken or if these were the wrong bugs. "I beg your pardon," said Ben flatly, "but you are supposed to be the Keepers of the Light, right?"

"Not 'supposed to be'. We *are* the Keepers of the Light."

"Where exactly do you keep it then?"

"Did you expect us to flash light from our rear ends as though we have no sense of decency or decorum?" answered the Elder haughtily. "I don't mean to sound crass, but tell me, how would mooning the Queen with a brilliant beam of bum light prepare the way for her return? Would you take that as an invitation to return home if you were her? I know I wouldn't. Your problem is you are far too literal. Light, in this case, is a symbol for something else, something that brings clarity and chases darkness from our lives. Can you guess what it stands for?"

Ben was puzzled and his expression conveyed as much without saying a word. The Elder picked up on Ben's confusion and gave a hint: "The Light has been on display already tonight." Ben only blinked at him, so he explained. "The rules. We have been chosen to keep the rules—the Queen's rules—and we must see to it that others do too. Misdeeds and rule-breaking by the bugs in this garden drove the Queen away; only when every bug follows her rules again will she come back."

"What about Ramsay?" asked Ben. "Why would he allow you to enforce the Queen's rules instead of his?"

"Ramsay was once greatly concerned with us. He sent spies to live among us, and not even the aspens could keep them out. But one day, the spies departed, and he's left us alone ever since. We don't know why for certain, but we believe it was because he sensed the Queen's blessing upon us. And why has the Queen blessed us with a power even Ramsay fears? Simple—because we follow her rules. That is how powerful her rules are and why we must insist you follow them. Since you violated the rules tonight, we cannot help you. But I'm inclined to be lenient, so if you come back tomorrow before curfew, we'll reexamine your case then." The Elder, certain this was the last word, turned his back to Ben.

"But they need help now," said Ben firmly, stopping the Elder with his voice. "If we don't get to the Hive before dawn, they will die. Please tell me how to get them through the aspen grove."

"You just don't get it," said the Elder, fixing his vicious eyes on Ben. "Rules are rules, and more rule-breaking won't save anybody. It might seem harsh, but our love for the Queen requires us to be firm."

Ben's reply was calm, deliberate, and angry: "Don't you dare blame your indifference to whether they live or die on the Queen. She moved mountains for the love of her bugs, yet you won't lift a finger for them. You're content to sit there and let them die. For what? Curfew? Vehicle specifications? You're supposed to be the Keepers of the Light, but from where I'm sitting I can't tell the difference between you and the spiders."

"I'm warning you," growled the Elder, "your disrespect will cost you dearly, rule-breaker."

"And I'm warning you that your disregard for who the Queen really is will cost you."

"We honor the Queen in all we do. We're the only one's trying to make the garden good enough for her return."

"The Queen doesn't need you to make anything good enough for her to return. That's why Ramsay leaves you alone. Do you really think if you were going to bring back the Queen doing what you're doing he would just let you? No, he leaves you alone because you're doing his work for him. He uses his rules to crush us bugs, and so do you. You just dress it up a little differently."

"So her rules mean nothing to you?"

"Nothing was more important to her than her bugs. If following your rules keeps you from remembering that about the Queen, then you don't know the first thing about her. Now if you'll excuse me, my friends still need me." Ben turned his back on the elders and took Waverly and Oliver toward the aspen grove.

The Elder cursed and yelled at him as he left, but Ben never looked back. When Ben was gone, the hooded creatures who had sat noiselessly during the encounter circled around their leader. The Elder looked squarely at the cloaked figure who had been standing in the very back and said, "You're right; he is dangerous.

If he disregards the law that openly, surely nothing good can come of him."

Lowering the hood to show his face, Floyd replied, "Then do the right thing and help us. The spiders are ready to make a move. You just have to tell me where that one place is where they can make it through the aspen grove."

"Not through exactly, but there is a way to get to the other side. But they'll never find it."

"Ramsay wants to be ready in case they do."

"I don't know," said the Elder, uncertain Ben merited revealing his carefully guarded secret.

"Just think of what would happen if other bugs started thinking and acting like him. It would set you back years. Surely, you'd agree that he shouldn't be allowed to get away with speaking to a bug of your stature the way he did."

The Elder nodded, straightened his back, and filled his chest with air. "Such disrespect must not be tolerated."

Floyd smiled because he was about to get what he wanted.

***

After tromping across the field away from the elders, Ben marveled at the aspen grove in front of him. It had clearly earned its reputation of impassibility. Row after row of trees crowded so closely together that not even a blade of grass could squeeze between them. The grove stretched for as far as the eye could see in either direction. Ben walked alongside it looking for a breach, but found none. His hope diminished with every step.

Ben had taken every setback and humiliation in stride, but to have come all this way, to have suffered all he had only to be thwarted by a couple of trees was one burden too many to bear. To make matters worse, the only bugs who he thought could help him were the most decidedly unhelpful insects he ever met. His determination melted into desperation, and he unloaded his frustration on the nearest aspen tree, fists pounding, feet kicking as he howled into the night. Before long, he fell to his knees, exhausted, and sunk his head into his hands.

He raised his moist eyes to look at Waverly and Oliver and said, "I'm sorry. I did all I could ... I don't know what else to do. I'm so sorry." He put his hands on their shoulders and hung his head but could not get out another word.

Behind Ben, off in the distance, a soft light gently pulsed, cutting through the darkness. Waverly and Oliver both saw it over his shoulders. It faded away as quickly as it had come, but in another moment it was back. Every few seconds the light came and went, glowing faintly at first, swelling in brightness, then yielding back to the darkness.

Even though their bodies had failed them, Waverly and Oliver had not given up. They fought to let Ben know what was happening behind him, to tell him there still might be a chance. But when Oliver opened his mouth to speak, he could only manage a strange, goose-like honking noise. His loud "Ahnk!" startled Ben.

"Are you okay?" Ben asked.

All Oliver could do in reply was repeat himself more loudly. "Ahnk! Ahnk! Ahnk!"

Waverly did not fare much better. She was reduced to spitting out a high-pitched squealing sound. "Qui! Qui! Qui!"

"I can't bear to see you so sad. This is terrible." Ben threw his arms around them and tucked his head between their shoulders.

Waverly and Oliver rocked forward in their seats and stomped their feet on the cart. Ben jumped in surprise and pulled back to look at them. They honked and squealed even louder, all while keeping their eyes fixed on the pulsing light.

Finally, Ben turned around and stared into the darkness. He saw nothing at first. But after a moment of waiting and wondering what had gotten into his friends, the light flickered in the distance. After it faded away, he doubted what he had seen, then it blinked again.

He jumped off the cart and started pushing it toward the light, running as fast as his weary legs would allow. As he got closer, the lights grew more radiant, and he soon realized there were two lights pulsing in unison. The pace of their flicker remained steady, even as they started to move and bounce around. He drew closer still and heard singing and laughing. When he reached the source of the lights, he saw two fireflies dancing and frolicking in the air, their tails flashing effortlessly in perfect rhythm with their song.

Seeing Ben, they immediately stopped their dance to tend to him. "You've been crying," said one of the fireflies. "What's wrong?"

"My friends are dying."

"What can we do?" they asked, their lights still flashing rhythmically even though their song had stopped.

"They've been bitten by spiders. They'll die by morning unless I bring them to the Hive, but I can't find a way through the grove."

"That's because there is no way through it," said one of the fireflies. "You have to go under it to get to the Hive. Follow us— we'll show you." The fireflies took hold of the cart and pushed it alongside the aspen grove so quickly and effortlessly Ben struggled to keep up. "Why don't you hop on?" they asked.

Ben gladly took their suggestion and sat on the back of the seats between Waverly and Oliver. Looking down, he saw his friends bathed in a scatter of light from the fireflies. For the first time he realized, despite all that had happened to them, they still appeared content.

"You can call me Zeil," said the firefly on the left. "And this is Meesh."

"I'm Ben. These are my friends, Waverly and Oliver. Aren't you guys fireflies?"

"We aren't guys, but we sure are fireflies," answered Zeil.

"It's funny, I met some fireflies earlier, but they sure didn't act like you."

"What did they act like?"

"They were kind of mean, and they didn't light up like you do."

"Sounds like you met the elders," said Meesh. "They can be quite stern. They say fireflies shouldn't light up, that we should be more dignified than that."

"How do you get your tails to light up like that any way?"

"We don't really know," said Zeil. "They didn't used to glow."

"It just happened one day," Meesh explained. "Late one night, we were flying near the lake when we heard someone crying. We called out, and a bug answered. He told how he got caught in a spider web and if someone didn't help him, he'd be a goner. Our hearts just broke for him."

Zeil told the rest: "It was almost time for curfew, and, I'm sure you saw, the elders get very cross if you are out past curfew.

But we couldn't just leave this poor bug all alone; we had to help. So we looked and looked for him, but it was too dark to see. Slowly our tails started to glow, and by their light we were able to find him even though the world around us was pitch black. We pulled him loose before the spiders could get him, and our lights have been glowing ever since."

"Doesn't that make you the Keepers of the Light?"

"I don't know anything about that," answered Meesh. "We only knew you needed help like he needed help, so we got out where you could see our lights."

"I am glad you did," said Ben. "But how did you know I needed help?"

"It's a little weird, but ever since we found that bug in the web, not only do our tails light up, we can also hear the sound of crying anywhere in the garden," said Zeil.

"Most of the time we aren't close enough to do anything to help," continued Meesh. "The spiders keep us from getting too far from home. It was risky even getting out to help you."

"Speaking of home," said Zeil, stopping to set down the cart, "we're here."

Ben looked around trying to figure out where exactly their home might be and what distinguishing features existed to let them know they had arrived. To him it looked precisely like the rest of the grove.

Meesh removed a few leafy branches from the grove, allowing a soft, pulsating light to peak out. Clearing away more brush revealed a small opening, just wide enough for the cart. It was the entrance to a cave.

The path into the cave descended sharply, and Ben cringed remembering his last unfortunate trip down a hill so steep. Zeil and

Meesh sensed his apprehension. "Don't worry," they assured him, "we've got you."

As they went deeper into the belly of the cave, Ben sensed damp, cool air settling on his skin, a welcome change from the bitterly cold autumn night outside. The light grew more intense the closer they got to the source, so much so that Ben had to shield his eyes. Sounds echoed, but none more persistently than the gentle sound of tinkling water. Meesh explained, "This cave once housed the source of the Queen's underground river. It's only a small trickle now, but it's still here. You could see it if you looked."

When he raised his head, the light no longer hurt his eyes, and he found himself in a large cavern with high ceilings. Far above the stream burbling across the floor of the cave flew dozens of brightly lit lightning bugs who looked like an ever-changing kaleidoscope. Being in their presence made Ben feel warm and safe.

Zeil called out, "We're back, everybody, and we brought Ben. Waverly and Oliver are here too."

The fireflies gave a loud, friendly greeting to their guests. "We're ready for them," called one of the flying fireflies. "Let us know if they're ready for us." The fireflies went dark and stood still.

"You're very close to the Hive," Meesh told Ben. "You'll be there before you know it. But first, we've prepared something for you all, and we'd like to give it to you before you go. It shouldn't take too long. What do you say?"

"We'd love nothing more," said Ben, feeling strangely serene.

Meesh and Zeil pushed the cart against the back wall and tipped it so Waverly and Oliver could easily see the top of the cavern where the fireflies hovered.

"They're ready," shouted Meesh.

On cue, the fireflies performed a tightly choreographed light show in which they swirled, twisted, shimmied, and flipped high above the ground. It was beautifully planned and perfectly executed. As impressive as this display was, it was the finale that truly amazed.

The fireflies split into two groups and went to opposite ends of the cave. They flew, one at a time from each side, into the center of the room where they slammed into one another and an astonishing explosion of light filled the cave. The fireflies came away without injury and returned grinningly to their respective sides. One after another, in rapid succession, they collided in the middle of the cavern producing fantastic eruptions of light. When all the fireflies had gone, the sequences grew more complicated and even more wonderful. Two from each side, then four, then ten. They flew in pinwheels, then figure eights, all ending in a dazzling display of fireworks by firefly. The performance concluded when every firefly converged simultaneously on the center of the cave, leaving a blinding deluge of light in their wake.

At this last blast, Ben looked over at Waverly and Oliver and saw huge grins on their illuminated faces. It felt like he had not seen them smile in years.

"We hope you liked it," said Meesh. "It's our gift to you."

"I loved it," Ben replied, "and more importantly they loved it. Thank you."

After the light had fizzled out, Zeil turned serious and said, "It's time to go now. You'll have to leave the cart here. It won't fit where we have to take you, and you won't need it any more any way."

Ben was reluctant to leave the cart behind. Though it was battered and nearly broken, without it he never could have made it this far. But he too knew it was time to let it go.

Zeil and Meesh grabbed his arms as the other fireflies swept him up from behind. The rest lifted Waverly and Oliver over their heads, and they all moved toward the opposite end of the cave, toward the source of the once vital underground river.

"We have to warn you," said Meesh as she carried Ben, "if we let you go to the other side, we'll be delivering you into the spiders' hands. Normally, we would never allow that to happen, but we know that's why you've come."

"Whatever happens to us on the other side," said Ben, "I could never blame you for it; I'll only remember your kindness. I'm ready for what comes next."

The fireflies pressed on to the far end of the cave, where the ceiling was so low they could no longer stand up straight. After a tearful goodbye, the lightning bugs released Ben into a small, dark tunnel, and he slid into the unknown. The fireflies passed Waverly to the front of the pack and dropped her in after Ben. Oliver followed close behind. When they had all gone, the fireflies gave each other sad, knowing looks as their lights went dim.

CHAPTER EIGHTEEN
BEFORE THE HIVE

A tiny stream of water ushered the flies quickly through the tunnel. The glow of the lightning bugs had faded, leaving the flies twisting and turning in an unsettling darkness. They were stranded in this lightless world for a few moments until Ben, after rounding a corner, caught glimpse of an orange flickering light, which burned brighter at every turn. The tunnel came to an abrupt end and he shot into the air feet first, did half a flip, and landed face down in a sticky net suspended ten feet above the ground between two trees. Seconds later, Waverly and Oliver, one right after the other, ejected out of the opening and into the same web.

There was not a trace of either star or moonlight in the sky, only the menacing glow from torches carried by dozens of spiders. The quivering fires blurred the lines of where one spider stopped and the next began, turning them into a disembodied collection of furry backs, glistening fangs, and glowing eyes. The scene was reminiscent of that tragic morning in Diterra, but experiencing it by torchlight with the cobweb-draped Hive looming over them made it even more terrifying. The fact that neither Waverly nor Oliver could cry out reminded Ben why he had traveled so far to put himself in this position.

"You made it after all," said a familiar voice, rising out of the crowd and slicing through the dreadful silence. Ben focused his eyes on the voice, and slowly Noth emerged from the spider blob below. Behind Noth, Ben noticed Floyd sitting in a spindly tree.

"Noth!" said Ben.

"I'm flattered," said Noth sarcastically, "you remembered me."

"I'm here to see Ramsay."

"You just jump right into what you want to talk about, don't you? No 'Hello,' no 'how have you been?' You might be ill-mannered, but you are the most resilient bug I think I've ever seen. I am honestly surprised you made it this far after what you've been through. The only way we could have made it harder for you was if we would have killed you outright."

"Save the speech, Noth. I just need to see Ramsay."

"Nice to see you still lack the sense to know you are in no position to make demands," said Noth. "In all honesty, Ramsay is probably still sleeping. And just so we're clear, you won't be seeing him today."

"What?" Ben was livid. "What do you mean? They have to see him; they've only got an hour or two left!"

"Will you calm down. I only said *you* won't be seeing Ramsay today; your friends will get to see him. Or at least Ramsay will be seeing them—he has to eat after all."

With that, two spiders scaled the web toward the flies. The spiders lifted Waverly and Oliver's still bodies and began wrapping them in spider silk, starting at their feet and working up. Ben cried out for the spiders to stop but was only mocked for his pleading. Try as he might, he could not free himself from the web to help his friends. He could only wonder: *Did Waverly and Oliver know what was happening to them? Were they scared? Would they cry if they could?*

Around and around, the spiders turned them, coating them in a seemingly endless line of silk. Waverly and Oliver were slowly disappearing from sight. Soon all Ben could see of his friends was their tired, expressionless faces, which were covered with another line of silk every time the spiders rolled them over. Then another, and another, until finally, they were lost to him, lost behind peaceful white cocoons that belied the horror of it all.

The spiders dropped the two cocoons—one short and round, the other slightly taller and leaner—to their partners waiting below. Those on the ground collected the little bundles and eagerly whisked them away. Ben watched them as they went all the way to the entrance of the Hive. His head sunk when they vanished inside.

"Don't worry," teased Noth, "you'll get to where they're going someday—just not today. You've got too much life in you yet, but an extended stay at the Dung Heap should take it out of you."

Ben sat bitterly silent and alone on the web. Staring at the ground, in a raspy, barely audible voice, he asked, "Why?" All the pain he had endured was channeled into this one simple question.

"Because they broke Ramsay's rules. Because we felt like it. Because we could. Take your pick, who cares, what does it matter? There's nothing you can do for them now."

"That's what you say. I still need to see Ramsay. I promised them I would do whatever it takes to save them, and that means I can't stop until I've seen Ramsay ... face to face."

"Let me free you from your delusions: there never was anything you could do for them, Ramsay or no Ramsay. He simply needed to get you here, and your fanatical devotion to them made it possible. Ramsay received a prophecy that a rebellion would rise from Diterra. However, his prophet also revealed that Ramsay would defeat the rebel leader, but only if Ramsay could draw him to the Hive. We once thought you might have been that rebel leader, Ben. We needed to make sure you came to the Hive in a hurry, with no time to raise an army for your insurrection, so we poisoned your friends and told you there was a way to save them. You took the bait. The problem for you is there is nothing you can do for them. And the problem for us is that you're no rebel. Turns out, you're just a kook."

"How can you be so sure?" asked Ben. "What if I came here to put an end to Ramsay's rule?"

"What do you think I'll do, have second thoughts and rush you up to Ramsay? Nice try, but it's too late; we already know all about you. We put the means for rebellion in your path—the ants were ideal recruits for an army—but you rejected it. We gave you a chance to live like a king. But rather than enjoy the fruits of power, you tore down the termite's mound. Then we arranged a meeting with Ramsay's only publicly avowed enemies, and you insulted them. A real rebel wouldn't have passed up each of those chances, but you did. So don't pretend you're leading some big rebellion when you've already proven you're nothing but a little nut."

"At least Floyd reported back to you accurately," said Ben.

"Which reminds me—Floyd, could you come down here to let me express my gratitude?" Floyd casually flew to Noth's side, his pride swelling in anticipation of public praise. Noth wrapped his arms around Floyd's shoulder. "I want to thank you for your services," said Noth, pausing as he slipped his hands around Floyd's neck, lifted him off the ground and flung him into the web, "which are no longer needed!"

"What are you doing?" shouted Floyd, now ensnared on the opposite side of the web from Ben. "You can't do this to me!"

Ignoring Floyd completely, Noth said, "Really Beesley, I'm doing this for you. Since you like spending time with rule-breakers so much, we thought you'd love to spend your final days with one of the biggest I've ever seen."

"But I'm Ramsay's messenger. He'll never stand for this."

"These are Ramsay's orders, maggot," answered Noth. "He knows you were ready to turn on him. You can't be trusted anymore, so you're done." Noth turned his back on both of them and crawled off toward the Hive. As he scurried away, he barked out one last order: "Take them to the Dung Heap!"

CHAPTER NINETEEN
THE DUNG HEAP

On Noth's command, pairs of spiders mounted the web to retrieve Ben and Floyd. They bound the bugs' hands and feet together with spider silk then dropped them onto the rocks below. Although the impact knocked the wind out of him, Ben stayed calm as the spiders scooped him up and carried him away. In stark contrast, Floyd thrashed about, shouting curses at the spiders as he attempted to stab them with his proboscis. Many of the spiders hated Floyd and took great joy in silencing him by tying his tongue to his hands.

They were ushered past the entrance of the Hive and taken to a large yard that ran along its exterior. The yard was covered with a triple-layered, reinforced cobweb dome that prevented any chance of escape. A noxious odor made Ben gag when it met his nostrils. Inside the dome, steam rose off the filthy sludge that coated the ground and formed several oozing mounds throughout. There was no mistaking it: this was the dreaded Dung Heap.

Two burly spiders with matted hair emerged from a guard shack that sat outside the yard. One of the guards called, "Halt! Who comes there?"

"We come in Ramsay's service with more rule-breakers to throw on the Heap."

"Draw nigh." After the escorts brought their prisoners near, the guards inspected them closely. "What have we here?" asked one guard as the other teasingly tugged on Floyd's tethered tongue.

"A fly of medium build and a small mosquito, each jailed on Ramsay's direct orders. Feel free to be extra rough with both of them."

"You mean like this," said the guard as he effortlessly grabbed Ben and Floyd and rammed their heads together. "Should be fun. Wait here—be back in a second."

The guards slipped back into their shack. Once his head stopped ringing, Ben could hear them rummaging around, opening and slamming doors as they mumbled between themselves. When they emerged, each was holding a coat with yellow and black horizontal stripes.

"All right, this one's for a small mosquito," said the guard who threw the smaller coat at Floyd, who was still stunned from butting heads with Ben.

The other guard handed his coat over to Ben's captors adding, "And one fly, medium."

The spiders freed Ben and Floyd's hands one at a time to slip the coats on them. They laughed every time they made the bugs wince or say "ouch." Once the coats were on, the spiders stitched them closed with their silk. "Now everyone who sees you will know you've made enemies with Ramsay by your rule-breaking."

"Let's clip their wings," said one of the escorts, "then we'll be off."

"The wing-clipper is on break. Don't know when he'll be back," replied one of the guards.

"But we can't leave until they get their wings clipped, and we've got things to do."

"Clipper's had a real busy night with the last lot you brought us, so he could be a while. Why don't we just bind these two together until he gets back. That'll keep them on the ground and you won't have to stick around."

"Works for me."

The spiders stood Ben and Floyd back to back, wing to wing, and tied them together, wrapping them up so they could barely move, occasionally punching them in the gut or poking them in the eyes. With the bugs thoroughly secured, the spiders flung open a gate, which was the only movable portion of the dome and the only way in or out of the Dung Heap. The guards lifted the bugs by their arms and legs and tossed them unceremoniously into the sludge.

Ben and Floyd landed with a splatter as the gate slammed shut behind them. Globs of slop splashed into their eyes, drastically impairing their vision. Lying on their sides, bound together and sunken in mud, made it extremely difficult for them to get up. Every time Ben got close to standing, Floyd jerked in a different direction, and they both tumbled to the ground again. As they fought for control, they rolled through the mud repeatedly, each taking a turn to be face down in the muck.

When they had worn themselves out and come to rest on their sides again, Floyd spat with disgust. "Do you have any idea how bad this tastes?"

"Then stop rolling around already," said Ben. "If you would stop moving long enough, I could stand us both up."

Neither wanted to take another face-first dip in the sludge, so Floyd held very still while Ben pulled himself onto his knees, then rose to standing. Through the slop that coated their eyes, they saw a handful of bugs wearing the same yellow and black prison uniforms coming at them.

Ben raised Floyd off the ground when he bent his head down to his hands to wipe the gunk from his face. With his eyes cleared, the dozens of bugs who now surrounded them came into focus. They were sickly and hungry, looking like they had not eaten in weeks. A grasshopper and a horned-beetle stepped out of the crowd and grabbed hold of the silk wrapped around Ben and Floyd.

Talking about Ben like he was not there, the grasshopper said, "He's tied up and won't be able to fight back. I say we eat him."

"You read my mind," said the beetle.

"Sorry buddy," said the grasshopper, as he leaned in and fit his pincers around Ben's neck, "it's nothing personal; we're just starving." Ben leaned his head away from the grasshopper and gritted his teeth.

Suddenly, a bug screamed out, "That's enough!" A ripple coursed through the mob as the bug pushed his way to the front. Ben saw a flash of red as the bug burst forward and knocked the grasshopper to the ground. "I can't let you do that Dewpont. This is just what the spiders want us to do." The red bug spun around and took hold of the beetle's horn before it rammed him from behind. Forcing the beetle to the ground, the bug said, "Don't even think of it Tio."

Ben was shocked to see a familiar eye patch and bronze helmet on the bug who had just saved his life. "Colonel?" asked Ben. "Is that you?"

"Beesley?" asked Clausewitz as he stepped toward Ben in what was an intensely surreal reunion. "Have you seen Ramsay?"

"Not yet."

"Where are Waverly and Oliver?" asked someone else.

To his right, Ben saw two jacket-clad termites he recognized instantly as Zimra and Ulli. "The spiders took them into the Hive."

"Who knows Waverly and Oliver?" asked a stout creature working his way through the crowd. He looked like a spider but had only six legs. "Say, aren't you that fly they saved?"

"That's me. Are you the spider who let us go?" asked Ben.

"In the flesh—at least what's left of it," he said while rubbing the spots where two of his legs had been ripped from his body. He wore the same yellow and black jacket as the rest, but his was obviously two jackets that had been sewn together to accommodate his large, un-bug like shape. "Name's Dap."

"Sorry to find you here, Dap," said Ben. Just then, dozens of fireflies emerged from behind the mounds in the distance with Zeil and Meesh leading them. Their wings poked out through their prison jackets, and large triangle-shaped holes had been cut into their wings to keep them from flying. "Not you too," cried Ben.

"They came for us seconds after you left," explained Zeil.

Ben quickly realized that many of the bugs on the Dung Heap were there because they had helped him. Their acts of kindness were treated by Ramsay as acts of treason worthy of the most serious penalty.

"Sorry to break up the reunion," yelled Floyd, who had gone quiet while he successfully struggled to free his tongue from the knot that cinched it to his hands, "but would someone untie us?"

The other bugs had forgotten Floyd was there until his outburst. Clausewitz limped forward—he was still wearing the splint Ben had made for him—and slid his pincers around the spider silk that bound Ben and Floyd together, and cut them loose. Dewpont, who apparently had been talked out of eating them, cut through the spider silk on the other side.

While Ben wiped the sludge off his body, Floyd vented his frustration: "There must be some kind of mistake; I shouldn't be here. They're here out of the kindness of their dumb old hearts," pointing at Clausewitz and the termites. "But I certainly didn't help you, so what am I doing here? I made it harder on you. I spied on you. I should have been rewarded!"

"Every bug ends up here. Ramsay makes sure of it," said Ben. "He was never going to treat you any differently simply because you were loyal. To him, you were never anything other than a rule-breaking bug. Look around—this is your reward."

Ben looked up at the sky, which was now hinting at the dawn's approach. "Listen, Waverly and Oliver don't have much time left. It's probably less than an hour before the poison takes them. I have to get inside that Hive, but I'll need your help."

"Count me in," said Clausewitz without any hesitation, but the rest of the group stood there silently. Ben looked directly at each of the bugs, pleading with his eyes. They did not look back at him.

"What I'm asking you to do is frightening. Most bugs spend their lives avoiding spiders, doing their best to pretend like they don't really exist or hoping they'll always stay in the shadows. I'm asking you to stand up to them. You're on the Dung Heap because you broke Ramsay's rules. And you did, each and every one of you did. Everyone does at some point. It's inescapable. All of you were going to end up here one way or another. Ramsay has brought this curse on all of us. Waverly and Oliver are up first; they'll pay with their lives today. Tomorrow, it will be your turn. No matter what you do, you can't escape Ramsay's curse. So ask yourself, do you want to face Ramsay on your own tomorrow, or do you want to face him today with me?

"Before you answer, I want you to think about the bees who once made this Hive their home. They were wise. Kind. Brave. They loved each other and loved us. When they were here bugs weren't scared, and we lived in peace. Compare that to the garden you know: fear, anger, hate, despair. And here we are, in Ramsay's garden, trapped on his Dung Heap. Why? Because Ramsay rules even though this garden rightfully belongs to the Queen Bee. This hour, we can take it back for her. This hour, Ramsay's reign can come to an end.

"I'm asking you to take a side. The spiders don't want you on theirs. But look at your jackets. Yellow and black. What the spiders intended to shame us has instead made us allies with the bees. Wouldn't it be better if their love won out over the spiders' fear? Be like bees today, and Waverly and Oliver might be the *first* bugs rescued from Ramsay's cruelty. You can follow me or stay out here in the dung. It's up to you."

"I'm in," said Ulli.

"I'll do whatever you need me to," said Meesh.

"Me too," added Zeil. A chorus of fireflies chimed in behind them.

After a lengthy pause, Zimra added, "You can count on me, too."

"What I'm asking of you is no small thing," Ben said. "If you're not sure ..."

"No, I want to do it. I wouldn't be alive if not for you."

"What about you Dap?"

"I don't think you understand, Ben," said Dap meekly. "I've done some really terrible things to you bugs in my day. You're trying to do something good, but with what I've done, I'm afraid I might ruin it. I'd like to help, I would, but I'll only bring you down."

"I know you're a spider, Dap, even if you've only got six legs. Remember, I didn't ask you to be good, I only asked for your help. Will you help me?"

Dap had been staring down at the ground, but after a brief pause, he lifted his head and said, "I'd be honored."

"What do you say, Floyd?" said Ben, surprising everyone by extending the invitation to him.

"I don't know," answered Floyd, "I never really felt anything before. Then the spiders turned on me, and I was angry. Now, I feel lousy thinking about how your friends wouldn't even be in this mess if it weren't for me. Normally, I wouldn't care, but it's making me feel terrible."

"I knew you had a conscience, no matter how well you hid it. But if you don't follow it now, it might never bother you again."

"You should hate me. Why don't you hate me after what I did to your friends?"

"There's too much hate in this garden already. Why don't you help me instead?"

"Ok, I'll do it, but more to get revenge than to help you."

"Anybody else?" asked Ben.

With the exception of Dewpont, Tio, and a roly poly bug named Narv, who decided they would rather fight than wait to die, all the other bugs slipped away, opting to hide out in the back corner of the Dung Heap.

"Great," said Clausewitz, "you've raised your army, sad as it is. Now we need a plan of attack. Mosquito, you've seen the Hive from the inside—what's it like in there?"

"The most important thing to know," explained Floyd, "is that the throne room, where Ramsay spends most of his time, is on the side farthest from the entrance. Getting there is like going through a maze. And there are probably a hundred spiders on guard at any time, so we're a little outnumbered."

"Is there any way to get Ben to Ramsay?" asked Ulli.

"There might be. Every morning this creepy little cricket comes to tell Ramsay his fortune. Ramsay believes everything this guy says and is obsessed with keeping these meetings secret. He doesn't trust anybody, so he makes all the spiders except for the two guards outside his throne room clear out to at least the middle of the Hive. After the prophecy is given, the little creep disappears, and all the spiders take up their posts again. The way I see it, we've got a five minute window when Ramsay is as close to unguarded as he gets."

"I worked in the Hive before I was stationed to Diterra," added Dap. "Ramsay eats right after these sessions, and he likes his food fresh. If Waverly and Oliver were taken inside this morning, they'll be placed on Ramsay's web right after he wakes up."

"When do these sessions start?" asked Ben.

Floyd pointed east and said, "At sunrise."

"We've no time to lose," said Ben, gazing up at the brightening sky. "Listen closely, here's what I need you to do ...."

190

CHAPTER TWENTY
OPERATION UGLY HONEY

Deep within the Hive, Ramsay slept fitfully on his web. He jerked and twisted and waved his arms in front of his face as though he was swatting away an invisible attacker. Suddenly he popped awake, sat upright, and let out a gasp. Relieved to have woken, he found himself all alone with only the memory of his nightmare. Waiting until his breathing slowed, he called the guards who stood watch outside his barren lair.

The door to the throne room swung open, letting in the flickering torchlight and two nervous guards. "Send for Noth," bellowed Ramsay. "I want his report on last night's confrontation."

"Right away, our Lord," said the guards, keeping their eyes to the floor. They turned and motioned to someone through the doorway.

Noth, who had been waiting outside the throne room in anticipation of Ramsay's request, entered the chamber behind them. On their way out, the guards closed the door, shutting out the light and leaving only the red glow of Ramsay's eyes to provide illumination.

"Master," said Noth with his head bowed, "great is your name. I have come to report on last night's encounter by the aspen grove."

"You may rise," said Ramsay, stretching his arms. A conspicuous yawn revealed his long, venom-streaked fangs. "What happened last night with our little band of rebels?" Noth never would have guessed from Ramsay's dismissive tone the amount of sleep that had been lost over these rebels.

"We have deemed they pose no threat to your kingdom," answered Noth. "Specifically, there was no evidence Ben Beesley was leading any rebellion."

"How can you be so certain he's harmless? If you're wrong about this, you'll be demoted to lice colony warden," Ramsay hissed.

"Beesley brought no army with him and made no efforts to raise one at any point on his journey despite having numerous opportunities. He never displayed any real thirst for power, never spoke of rebellion. In fact, he was a bit of a bungler. We could only conclude he was no threat. But just to be safe, we sent him to the Dung Heap."

"Are you saying the prophecy was wrong then?" asked Ramsay icily.

"No sir," stammered Noth, realizing Ramsay was more concerned about this fly than he had let on. "Surely your prophecy is true, but perhaps the interpretation is wrong."

"You mean *my* interpretation is wrong," replied Ramsay.

"I didn't mean it that way, my Lord." Noth's voice was now quavering. "The interpretation is still right; we just had the wrong bug."

"Your boldness is overwhelming," said Ramsay. "But good enough. Surely, Beesley's no threat to me now. What about Floyd?"

"He's on the Dung Heap with Beesley."

"That's good to know. I received a disturbing message and ... and he just couldn't be trusted anymore. Before I send you away, where are the children?"

"They're here, sir—wrapped and ready to eat. May I bring them in for your breakfast?"

"You may," Ramsay replied.

Noth's spiders entered the throne room with Waverly's and Oliver's well-wrapped bodies. "On my web," ordered Ramsay. "After you leave, let Croda know I am waiting for the word he has for me today. I have a feeling we will be turning our attention back to Diterra before the day is through."

***

"All right, last time: everybody knows their part?" asked Ben as he scanned his fellow prisoners' anxious faces. The remnants of night were being chased into the west by the light blues and pale oranges that precede the sunrise. "Any questions?"

"I've just one," said the Colonel. "What's the name of this operation? The code word that sums up the entire plan? Every good operation has one."

"How about," said Ben, thinking aloud, "Operation Ugly Honey?"

"It'll do in a pinch."

"Good, because Operation Ugly Honey starts now!"

Clausewitz led Dewpont, Tio, Narv, and most of the fireflies into the middle of the Dung Heap while the rest of the bugs gathered around the outer wall of the Hive. Hidden in a nook between two large mounds, Ulli and Zimra marked a spot on the Hive and girded themselves for what they were about to do. Doubts about Floyd and Dap's honesty surged to the fore of Ulli's mind. She exhaled loudly and wondered if they were walking right into a trap. Zimra put her hand on Ulli's shoulder and, as though she had read her sister's mind, said, "Ben trusts them. We can too."

"That's good enough for me," answered Ulli. "Let's go." Together, the sisters sunk their powerful jaws into the side of the Hive and chomped. In less than a minute they had chewed a hole large enough to walk through.

It was pitch black inside, so the termites stepped out of the way and Meesh slipped in, cautiously lighting up the lonely hallway. It was just as Dap and Floyd said it would be on the side of the Hive where the throne room was located: dark and empty, without a spider in sight. Meesh poked her head out to whisper, "All clear."

Ben smiled knowing he had been right about Dap and Floyd. "Everybody in," he called out as he dove into the Hive. Floyd, Dap, Zeil, and five of the lightning bugs followed close behind. Ulli and Zimra stayed outside and repositioned the sludge mounds to hide the hole they had made.

Inside, the fireflies provided the light while the bugs huddled together. "Two of you lightning bugs are coming with me and Floyd to head off the prophet before he gets to Ramsay's throne room. Dap, take Zeil, Meesh, and the rest of the fireflies to the control room to see what you can do about locking the spiders out, assuming the Colonel's team is able to do their part."

"Aye-aye, boss," said Dap.

"Remember what you're fighting for," said Ben as the group split in two. Ben and Floyd each scooped up a wing-clipped firefly and flew toward the throne room. Ben moved with such confidence and purpose that Floyd, who was supposed to be leading them through the maze of hallways, had a hard time keeping up.

***

Back out on the Heap, Clausewitz and his team unearthed a small catapult he had fashioned using sticks he found within the yard and some twine he kept hidden under his helmet. They rolled the catapult out of hiding, loaded it, and aimed it at the entrance to the Dung Heap.

After making a few last second adjustments, Clausewitz gave Ulli the all clear. She raced toward the front entrance, screaming, "They got out! They got out!"

"I can't look," stated Zimra as she watched her sister through partially covered eyes.

The guards came running out of the shack. "Who got out?"

"The mosquito and the fly," she answered. "They got out of their restraints and flew away through a hole in the dome."

"I knew this would happen—should have waited for that wing-clipper."

"You better sound the alarm and get in here," said Ulli, perhaps too eagerly.

One of the guards turned to the other and said, "If we ring the alarm, this will all be on our heads."

"I'm with you," answered the other guard. "Let's see if we can fix it quietly before getting the whole Hive involved."

Ulli was panicking. Ben's plan counted on the guards sounding the alarm and the spiders rushing out of the Hive to assist with the emergency in the yard. If the spiders stayed inside, Ben might not be able to get to the throne room.

Just then, she noticed one of the spider's hands resting on the gate, as though he had started to open it but had second thoughts. She knew she had to raise the stakes so she bent over and bit the guard's hand. He shrieked in pain, and Ulli turned and ran back toward Clausewitz and his platoon.

The guards flung the gate open and chased after her. They were so single-mindedly focused on running her down, they failed to notice Clausewitz's fortifications in the distance. Even though the Colonel had the spiders in his sights, they were dangerously close to Ulli and he risked hitting her too if he fired the catapult now. Yet if he did not do something soon, Ulli would be overtaken.

Zimra could not bear to watch anymore. She sprang forward, yelling, "I'm going in after her." With her head lowered and her arms pumping, she charged as hard and fast as she could toward Ulli and the spiders.

Clausewitz prepared his troops: "Steady boys. Fire only on my command." They watched Zimra race across the yard, kicking up slop as she went.

"Hold," ordered Clausewitz. One of the spiders reached out his foreleg to take a swipe at Ulli. He missed, but just barely; she even felt him brush against her jacket.

"Hold!"

Ulli looked up to see her sister charging toward her and the spiders. A split second later, Zimra leapt off her feet and took Ulli down with a flying tackle. They tumbled head over feet as the spiders zipped past them. Zimra's stunt gave Clausewitz the opportunity he had been waiting for.

"Fire!" The fireflies eagerly launched the catapult, which flung tightly compacted balls of sludge into the air. Before the payload even landed, the troops reloaded, repositioned the catapult slightly, and fired off another round.

Realizing they had overshot the termites, the spiders skidded to a stop, spraying up slop with their braking feet. Before they could step back toward Zimra and Ulli, a sludge ball landed with disgusting fury on the spider Ulli had bitten. The termites ducked for cover as mud splattered everywhere. When they looked up to survey the damage, another sludge ball landed in the middle of the other spider's back. Daring to raise their heads again, Ulli and Zimra saw both spiders lying motionless, still breathing but unconscious.

The first phase of Operation Ugly Honey had not gone as planned, but with both guards knocked out and the gate left wide open, it would be easy to get back on track.

***

By the light of the fireflies, Dap led his crew through a maze of hallways toward the center of the Hive. But as they rounded the corner of one hallway, they noticed the glow of torchlight at the other end. Where there was torchlight, there were spiders. Dap recoiled, pulling everyone back around the corner. The fireflies hid their light and filled with worry that the spider had already seen them. At first there was silence. Then the sound of eight legs gently tapping against the ground slowly came closer and closer as the torch's glow filled up more of the hallway.

"He's coming this way. All right, just like we talked about. Meesh, Zeil take your places. Everyone else fall in behind me."

Zeil and Meesh latched onto Dap's side, disguising themselves as his missing arms. It was not perfect, but in the dim light, Dap looked fully like a spider again. They clenched their jaws and waited for the confrontation to begin.

"Hello," said a solitary spider as he rounded the corner with torch in hand. "What are you doing here?"

"Doing a perimeter sweep for security preparedness," Dap answered.

"Nobody is permitted beyond my post at this hour. Ramsay is receiving his prophecy soon."

"Sorry, I forgot all about that. Just transferred back to the Hive after a tour in the field—must have slipped my mind."

"Don't let it happen again," replied the guard. "I saw a light. Where did your torch go?"

"Aaaah, I must have set it down," stated Dap, who had nothing he could pass off as a torch. He knew the game was almost up.

The guard's face reflected his concern. "Are you wearing a jacket?"

"Oh, the jacket—part of a new program to ah ... to ahh ... hey, there's my torch. Where did you find it?" Dap reached out for the guard's torch and knocked it from his hands.

"What did you do that for? Are you some kind of idiot?"

"My mistake. I can be such a klutz. Obviously that's your torch. Let me get it for you." Dap bent down toward the torch and planted his foot right on the flame. His foot might have been burned, but snuffing out that light was the only thing that mattered to him at the moment.

"There's no new program ..." muttered the guard to himself.

Dap whispered to Zeil and Meesh, "Flashers ready—as soon as I stand up."

"Wait, you're that spider who's on the Dung Heap," said the guard, not realizing it was already too late.

Suddenly, two electric flashes sizzled through the darkness. The guard grew dizzy and dropped to his knees. Zeil and Meesh's light had blinded him. Before he could call out for reinforcements, Dap clubbed him over the head with his own torch and wrapped him up in spider silk.

"Well done, ladies," Dap said. "Let's go. There are about three or four more checkpoints between here and the control room."

The fireflies kept their lights off as they crept through the Hive, following the winding hallways toward the next torchlight they saw. Dap approached each checkpoint with Zeil and Meesh at his sides while the rest of the lightning bugs stayed hidden from sight. After asking for help lighting the torch he had taken from the first guard, Dap whacked the next guard over the head too. They repeated this method of attack at each of the checkpoints until they reached the room that housed the controls to the gates. The controls, though, were on the opposite side of the room. Meesh peeked around the corner to find fifty of the nastiest looking spiders she had ever seen between them and their target. She quickly ducked back into the hallway with the others.

"What did you see?" asked Zeil.

"Let's just say we didn't plan on this. That room is still full of spiders."

Ben and Floyd clung to the ceiling of the Hive, each clutching a firefly in his hands and trying hard not to move. Below them, a dozen or so spiders paced back and forth along the hallway. Most carried torches, and all were searching for the intruders whose light they had seen. One of the hallways that was supposed to be empty was instead packed with spiders—an extra precaution devised by Ramsay in his paranoia. Ben and Floyd had nearly run right into them on the way to Ramsay's throne room. Even though the bugs were pinned down with nowhere to go, none of the spiders had noticed them on the ceiling.

Floyd leaned over to Ben and whispered, "I don't know why they're still here. They should have cleared out by now. You got to believe me." Floyd, for whom lying came so naturally, was greatly concerned about his credibility now that he was telling the truth.

"Don't worry, Floyd," answered Ben, "I trust you. I just hope everything is all right outside. Let's give them another minute, but if nothing changes, we're going to have to make a break for it."

"If they don't clear out, there's no way we'll make it to the throne room."

***

Back outside, Ulli and Zimra ventured beyond the gate the guards had left open and entered the shack. Within, they found all the tools used by prisoners performing hard labor on the Dung Heap—shovels, picks, wheelbarrows, and more. They hurriedly armed their regiment with the tools, and Clausewitz gave his army tips on how to make the most of their newfound weapons. With everyone armed and ready, Ulli and Zimra stepped back outside and pulled the alarm, which filled the Hive with the sound of wildly ringing bells.

The Colonel braced his troops for the impending onslaught: "My bugs of fire, my flies of lightning: Today we fight for life, and we'll only get one chance. Let's crown these spiders with smoke and thunder."

A moment later, a horde of spiders poured out of the Hive and toward the yard. Seeing their fallen comrades covered in sludge filled them with rage, but they could only get two spiders at a time through the gate. The catapult snapped, hurling its ammunition right into the first wave of spiders, who fell at the foot of the gate. Another pair of spiders tried to enter, but the bugs fired the catapult again.

Many spiders fell before a small group broke through the entrance and charged after Zimra and Ulli, who still had not made it back across the Dung Heap to the rest of their army. The termites let these lead spiders draw close to them and led them toward one of the sludge mounds. Narv, the roly poly bug, rolled down the side of the mound, crashed into three of the spiders and sent them sprawling. Two spiders managed to stay on Ulli and Zimra's heels. Suddenly, Tio, the horned-beetle, leapt out from behind the mound and rammed into the spiders' sides. Dewpont, the grasshopper, jumped from one spider's back to another's ensuring that each no longer posed a threat.

The catapult kept firing, but there were simply too many spiders to keep at bay. They were breaking through with greater success and soon there were more spiders on the Dung Heap than bugs. But as the spiders pushed past the mounds, they were met with the swinging shovels of well-concealed fireflies. Spiders suddenly found their legs being swept out from under them or a painful knot rising from their forehead. Fireflies riding in wheelbarrows held out rakes like they were lances as they crashed into spiders, consistently getting the better of them.

All across the Dung Heap, the spiders walked into trap after trap. Clausewitz's army had the spiders disoriented and in disarray. Ben's plan was back on track, and even going a little better than anticipated.

***

As Dap and the fireflies tried desperately to figure out a way to get across the room to the controls for the gates, alarm bells began clanging madly. The noise was so loud it made the Hive shake. When they poked their heads around the corner to see how the spiders were reacting, they saw them pouring out of the room toward the entrance to the Hive.

"Now's our chance!" shouted Dap. They dashed across the room to the controls where the only two spiders in the room remained.

"You're being relieved of duty," said Dap. All of the lightning bugs flashed in unison, again disorienting the spiders as Dap swung the burned out torch at both. They fell to the ground on top of each other as Meesh and Zeil flipped controls. Throughout the Hive, enormous gates with huge spikes on the bottom fell from the ceiling and plunged into the ground. The spiders who had rushed outside were now locked out.

***

The spiders hunting for Ben and Floyd cleared out of the hallway to answer the alarm. With them and their torches gone, the halls fell into darkness again.

"Come on," said Ben, dropping from the ceiling and flying in the direction they had been traveling before the spiders trapped them. "Looks like we might make it to the throne room after all."

CHAPTER TWENTY-ONE
FACE TO FACE

"If this area has been cleared, it means Ramsay already sent for the prophet," Floyd explained to Ben as they flew through a vacant chamber. "The only spiders left will be the two standing watch outside his throne room."

"Then we have to stop the prophet before he gets in sight of those guards," said Ben. "Hurry!"

"He always goes by way of Ramsay's trophy room. We should be there in a few more turns," said Floyd. Ben raced ahead of Floyd, who called out directions from behind.

They shot down another long hallway and Ben asked of a doorway on their left, "Isn't this the way?"

"No, keep going straight!"

But Ben did not listen. He abruptly stopped at the door, and Floyd zipped by him down the long corridor.

"Ben!" yelled Floyd. "What are you doing? Come on!"

"No, this *is* it," Ben said, half talking to himself and half responding to Floyd. "This way!" He turned left through the doorway.

"No!" hollered Floyd. "Where are you going? I know the way, you nut!"

Despite Floyd's protest, Ben showed no sign of slowing or turning and soon was out of sight. "I don't believe this. I'm sticking my neck out for him, and he pulls this?" said Floyd. "Looks like it's up to me and you, firefly. If we find the prophet, we'll have to hold him until Ben finds us."

***

Dap and his crew were surprised by their success. Not only had nearly every spider rushed out of the Hive in response to the alarm, the spiders who had been searching for Ben and Floyd raced by them heading for the exit. With a few seconds more and a flip of a switch, these spiders too would have been locked out. But suddenly, the last spider in the group stopped for no apparent reason. "It's a trick," he muttered to himself. Turning to see the bugs, he shouted, "Prisoners in the Hive! Prisoners in the Hive!"

Zeil stepped forward to try and intercept the spider as he raced toward them. He shot a strand of silk in her direction, and she dropped to the ground. "Duck!" she yelled to her friends. Dap and the fireflies all dropped to the ground only to realize too late that the spider was aiming not at them but at the controls. He yanked his silken thread and set off a different alarm, one that alerted the spiders that Ramsay was in danger.

Dap jumped to his feet to silence the alarm, but the damage had been done. In a flash, the spiders blew by them, headed toward Ramsay's throne room.

"We can't let them warn Ramsay," called Dap.

"Wouldn't Ramsay have heard the alarm?" asked Zeil.

"There are no alarms near the throne room anymore," answered Dap. "He doesn't like to have his sleep disturbed. If we don't stop them, they could get to Ramsay before Ben does."

Dap and the lightning bugs ran as fast as they could after the spiders. It was the first time in the history of the garden that bugs chased after spiders instead of the other way around.

***

Floyd zigzagged with his firefly through a couple of very quick turns, then entered the trophy room. To his surprise, on the opposite side of the room, Floyd saw Ben sitting on top of a heap and Ben's firefly standing nearby with his light shining brightly. As Floyd rushed in, he noticed two spiders at the bottom of the pile, each bound up with spider silk. Ben had the prophet pinned down on top of the spiders by holding tightly onto his purple robes. He had caught the prophet just in time—only two more turns and he would have made it to Ramsay's throne room.

"Glad you made it, Floyd," said Ben coolly. "Help me get him to his feet and let's get that robe off him."

"What happened here?" asked Floyd as he pulled Croda off the heap.

"We flew up behind them in the dark and knocked into one of his spider guards. We didn't know he'd have his own guards. When they turned around to see what hit them, we blinded them with a firefly flash. The spiders shot at us but were so disoriented, they tied each other up accidentally. I tackled the prophet, and we fell on top of the spiders. Then you showed up."

"But how did you know about that shortcut? I didn't even know about it."

"It just came back to me," said Ben. "I can explain later, but now we have to focus on Ramsay." He pulled the robes off the prophet, revealing an old bug with shriveled skin and vacant white eyes.

Floyd stepped behind Croda, jammed his proboscis up against the prophet's neck and said, "I haven't eaten in days, and I'm real hungry. So help me, if you say even one word, I'm off my diet pal."

Ben slipped Croda's cloak over his own head and pulled up the hood. It covered him from head to toe, and the hood cast a long shadow that hid his face. "How do I look?" he asked.

"Creepy enough to have fooled me," replied Floyd. "Now get in there."

Ben took a deep breath and headed off to meet Ramsay. After rounding a couple of corners, he saw the entrance to the throne room. Rather than scrutinizing and questioning him as Ben had expected, the guards simply stepped out of his way and allowed him to walk right in. It did not seem possible to Ben that after all he had been through, he was about to come face to face with Ramsay at last.

***

Clausewitz's troops had done better than expected. They had created the diversion that allowed Ben to get to the throne room and shocked themselves with their success in taking out the spiders. But shortly after they dispatched the first wave, reinforcements arrived. The element of surprise had been lost, and the spiders' superior numbers swung the battle in their favor.

With their own traps set, the spiders managed to chase or lure the fireflies into freshly woven webs. They shot strands of silk around the weapons raised by the Colonel's foot soldiers, ripping them away and leaving the fireflies defenseless. They disabled the wheelbarrows and overran and dismantled the catapult.

When the spiders caught Narv, they wrapped him up in a ball and kicked him around the yard. They tied Tio's horn to Dewpont's back legs, making it so neither could defend themselves when the spiders closed in around them. The spiders shot globs of silk around Ulli and Zimra's jaws and forced them into webs.

Clausewitz was the last bug standing. It took no fewer than six spiders to wrestle him to the ground. Even then he took off a few legs until they managed to tie his pincers together. They bit him repeatedly and tossed him into a web. With Clausewitz's defeat, the Dung Heap rebellion ended like every uprising before it: the spiders had prevailed. The bitter wind blew, and the sun's golden beams peaked over the horizon.

***

Ben's eyes immediately fixed on the two white cocoons suspended on the web above Ramsay's throne. He knew Waverly and Oliver were trapped within. Their only hope of getting out rested completely with him. He was so focused on his friends, Ben barely paid attention to his surroundings. It was only when Ramsay spoke that Ben was forced to pay attention to him—the final, most considerable obstacle of his journey.

"What words of warning and wisdom have you brought for me today, my prophet?" asked Ramsay with a growl as he lowered himself from his web to sit upon the throne. His red eyes gleamed and venom dripped from his lips. Ramsay appeared more gruesome and dangerous than Ben had imagined. "Is there a reason you do not approach the throne today?"

Ben had been so overcome by the sight of Waverly and Oliver on the verge of becoming Ramsay's breakfast, he had frozen in place. He collected himself quickly and, imitating the cricket's voice as best he could, said, "Only because today's word is a dire warning."

For a brief moment, a look of fear flashed across Ramsay's face. Ben saw it, but was it a reaction to the message or a realization that the messenger was an impostor? "If it's a message you must deliver," said Ramsay, "then come close and tell me just as you have seen."

Ben approached the throne, hoping to glide up the stairs like the prophet but happy to settle for hiding his limp. With his eyes on Waverly and Oliver, he whispered, "Hang in there. I'm coming for you." He crossed the raised platform and stopped in front of Ramsay's throne, directly underneath the cocoons.

"What truth have you come here to reveal today?" asked Ramsay. He tapped his legs impatiently against the throne.

Unlike Croda, Ben never bowed to Ramsay. Instead, he lifted his head, looked right at him, and in his own steady voice said, "You will set your captives free or your reign ends today."

Without missing a beat, Ramsay slid off his throne and came toward Ben. "Prophet," he snarled, "yesterday you revealed that my messenger would become his—should you have said instead that *the rebel* would become my messenger?" Ramsay jammed one of his legs into Ben's chest. "What I really think I'll take away from today's message," said Ramsay as he flicked Ben's hood off to reveal his face, "is your head!"

Ben backed toward the stairs. "Just so the message is clear," said Ben while slipping off the purple cloak to reveal his bee-striped prison shirt underneath, "you are not being asked, and I'm not begging. I'm giving you only one chance to let my friends go."

"So Noth was wrong about you. What a brazen rebel you turned out to be after all," said Ramsay shaking his head. "If only you had known about the real prophecies, then you might not have been so stupid as to confront me in my home." Ramsay suddenly exploded toward Ben, striking him across the face with one of his spear-like legs and knocking him to the ground.

Ben rolled to his back and defiantly stood back up. "This is not your home; the Hive and that throne belong to the Queen."

"How dare you speak her name to me!" roared Ramsay. He charged at Ben and rammed him down a flight of stairs. Ben tumbled down to the landing on the staircase, slamming against the wall before coming to a stop. He saw the spider's red, raging eyes at the top of the stairs as Ramsay said, "I'm actually glad you made it this far, Ben, because I wouldn't be able to rip you to pieces if you hadn't. My only regret is your little buddies aren't able to watch me do it."

Ramsay was talking so loudly the guards looked into the throne room to investigate. He waved them off and pulled a lever that released two large stones with a thick spider web between them from the ceiling. The boulders rolled down a track until they came to a crashing halt in front of the throne room doors. The web stretched across the entryway, guaranteeing no one could get in or out of the room and reducing the guards to the role of spectators. With the door barricaded, Ramsay knew he had Ben all to himself. He wiped some spit from his lips and leaped off the steps toward Ben.

Dap and the fireflies chased the spiders until they were exhausted. But with Dap's stout body and the lightning bugs' short legs, they could not catch up to keep them from getting to the throne room.

Then, without warning, the spiders turned and ran right at the bugs. They had seen that Ramsay's throne room was barricaded. Believing their king to be safe inside, they turned their wrath against the invaders. Soon, the spiders subdued the fireflies, wrapped them in silk, and cast them onto webs. They mercilessly tortured Dap and hung him by his feet when they were done. Having routed their enemies, the spiders headed to the throne room to watch Ramsay annihilate the leader of this rebellion.

Floyd heard the throne room gate drop into place. During his time in the Hive, he had seen that gate lowered only twice, both times because Ramsay wanted to mete out an unusually cruel punishment to bugs unfortunate enough to be brought to him in person. A few moments later, he could tell that a mob of spiders arrived at the gate to cheer on Ramsay. Floyd wondered what had happened to Dap and his crew and whether he was the last bug who would have any chance of helping Ben.

Floyd said to the fireflies, "I have to see what's going on. You stay with the prophet. You flash him if he makes one false move—got it?"

Floyd zipped around the corner. The spiders gathered around the throne room entrance were too enthralled watching Ramsay on the attack to notice Floyd as he forced his way between them to the front where he could see. Seeing Ramsay filled Floyd with anger. Seeing what Ramsay was doing to Ben made him burn. He tried to squeeze through the gate's webbing, but it was impassable. There was nothing he could do but watch and wait.

***

Ramsay sprung off the top step toward Ben. With his legs splayed out in all directions, Ramsay looked enormous compared to Ben's slight and broken body. Ben rolled off the landing and down another flight of stairs, narrowly avoiding being crushed. He hit the ground so hard it knocked the wind out of him and left him gasping for air.

Ramsay gave Ben no time to gather himself. He had just gotten back on his feet when Ramsay jumped from the second flight of steps, striking Ben across his face on the way down and knocking him onto his back.

"Do you know what irritates me the most about your kind?" asked Ramsay, a second before backhanding Ben's jaw. "I have spent my entire life in pursuit of greatness." Ben scrambled to his feet and backed his way toward the gate. "And I've driven away a greedy, arrogant, insufferable Queen." Ramsay kept pressing in, taking a swipe at Ben that barely missed. Ben kept backing away, trying in vain to increase the distance between himself and Ramsay. "And you want to bring her back. You refuse to acknowledge that I am greater than she ever was or ever could be." Ramsay shot a strand of silk around Ben's ankles. With a firm tug on the silk, Ramsay dropped Ben to the ground in front of the gate. The salivating spiders cheered for their master.

Ben rose to his knees only to find the spear-like tip of Ramsay's foreleg pointed at his face. "But I will forgive all and even free your little friends if you would for once acknowledge that I am greater than that Queen Bee you admire so much."

Ben, his chest heaving, silently stared at Ramsay.

"Well? Don't sit there like a dummy. What do you say, fly?"

"I would rather die."

"Let it be known that I gave you the chance to save your friends, but you refused to take it. Their blood is on your hands." Ramsay lunged at Ben with his dagger of an arm. Ben dodged a fatal blow by falling backwards, away from the spider. Though the blade failed to pierce Ben's skin, it caught his prison uniform at the midsection and sliced right through it, all the way up the neckline.

Ramsay recoiled. The crowd of spiders let out a collective gasp at the sight of what was underneath Ben's jacket. Although his prison garb had been ripped away, Ben's body was covered in yellow and black stripes, just like a bee's.

A mix of rage and horror swelled within Ramsay, but before he could act, he felt a sharp, stinging sensation on his backside. When Ramsay stepped away from Ben, he had backed into the gate, directly in front of Floyd. The mosquito, in the first heroic act of his life, sank his proboscis deep into Ramsay's flesh, managing to taste blood before the spiders pounced on him.

"Don't kill him," hissed Ramsay, facing his spiders. "Save him for me." When Ramsay turned around, Ben was gone. Floyd had bought Ben just enough time for him to get away.

"Up there!" the spiders cried out. "On the web!"

Ramsay looked up and saw Ben flitting through the air, struggling to keep his damaged wings moving him toward Waverly and Oliver. While irritated that Ben had slipped away, Ramsay could not help but smile; if Ben touched the web with as much as an antenna, he would be trapped. Ramsay raced up a wall, keeping his eyes on his prey.

As Ramsay climbed, Ben landed between the two white cocoons and put his hands on each of them. "It's almost over," he whispered, "you'll be free soon." Ben's feet were already stuck; there would be no getting off the web.

Grabbing Waverly's cocoon first, Ben pulled and tugged and strained until at last he pried it free. He cradled it in his arms, gave her a kiss, then carefully dropped it onto the purple robe that lay in a heap beneath them. As he turned toward the other cocoon, his side touched the web and it too was stuck. This made it much more difficult to pull Oliver's cocoon loose, but with incredible exertion and determination, Ben soon freed him from the web as well. Ben held Oliver briefly, kissing him before dropping his cocoon next to Waverly's.

Ramsay stepped onto the web even as Oliver's cocoon was falling to the ground. When Ben saw it had landed safely, he lay down on his back in utter exhaustion.

Ramsay crawled across the web and on top of Ben. Staring Ben in the face, he said, "Congratulations. You have given your friends about a minute longer to live than if you had never raised a finger for them. I do hope it was worth it, especially since you won't be around to live it with them. You see, your ridiculous quest to help your little maggot friends has come to an end. Now so must you."

Rearing back on his hind legs, Ramsay opened his mouth wide. Venom dripped from his fangs and splashed Ben's face. With his teeth aimed directly at Ben's neck, Ramsay lunged.

As Ramsay came surging toward him, Ben summoned his remaining strength and tried to lift his tail off the web. Normally, no bug would be strong enough to free himself from a spider's web, and especially not Ramsay's. However, Ben's prison uniform, the uniform Ramsay had sliced from the midsection up, hung around his waist, buffering his lower body from the web's grip. He raised his tail up high and pointed it at Ramsay's chest.

Instantly, Ben felt the full weight of the spider crashing down on his tail. Ramsay's teeth stopped an inch from Ben's neck—close enough for him to smell Ramsay's putrid breath.

The gleeful look on Ramsay's face turned to utter shock and devastation. He knew his worst fears had come true. He knew his reign had come to an end. Ramsay opened his mouth to speak but only groaned.

Ben felt a burning sensation in his tail after Ramsay tumbled onto the web next to him. Turning his head, Ben saw the bottom of a stinger protruding from the spider's chest. He gazed down at his tail to find the remnant of a broken-off stinger that matched perfectly with the one sticking out of Ramsay. Ben Beesley did not just look like a bee; he *was* a bee. And he had just stung Ramsay right through the heart.

Chapter Twenty-Two
Back Home Again

The spiders watching by the gate fell into bewildered silence, unable to comprehend what they had seen. Ramsay always won, and he had been winning only seconds ago. Even as it was unfolding they did not trust their senses. How could a broken-down fly transform into a bee and then sting Ramsay on his own web?

Ramsay was even more dismayed than his spiders were. He mustered the strength to speak. "But the prophecy ... how could this have happened?"

"Victory was promised to him who fought closest to home," replied Ben. "This Hive was my home first."

This truth came as surprisingly to Ramsay as Ben's stinger had. Convinced of his defeat, Ramsay collapsed onto his back and let out one last gasp. His legs stopped kicking and curled up tight under his body. What was unthinkable a moment ago had come to pass. Ramsay was dead.

Within seconds of Ramsay's last breath, one of the corners of his web detached from the wall. Without proper support, that side of the web sagged, causing Ramsay's body to roll away and fall. It landed face down in front of his old throne.

One after another, all the web's moorings came loose. Ben, who was still stuck, rode the web as it floated to the ground. It fluttered, swinging back and forth through the air, until it draped over the throne. Then Ramsay's web slowly melted away, leaving only tiny water droplets in its place. When it had dissolved completely, Ben was left resting on the seat of the throne.

He slumped over to lay his head on the armrest as he watched every web Ramsay had ever made begin to disappear. Within a minute, Ramsay's lair looked surprisingly bright and clean, as though it had never been blighted by his presence. Even the webbing on the throne room gate melted away. Knowing there was nothing between them and Ben overwhelmed the spiders with fear. Rather than attempt to avenge Ramsay's death, they ran away.

Throughout the Hive, outside on the Dung Heap, and across the whole garden, the same thing happened: wherever a web had been spun, it disappeared from sight. Anyone who had been caught up in a web was being set free. Dap and the fireflies were freed in time to see the spiders rushing out of the Hive. From the Dung Heap, Clausewitz and the others watched the spiders scatter in every direction, looking for places to hide.

The bugs on the Dung Heap walked right into the now strangely deserted Hive, met up with their friends, and found the throne room where Floyd was waiting for them. From the doorway, they saw the two little white cocoons resting on a purple robe on the elevated platform.

They watched the cocoons, waiting for something to happen. It was taking a very long time considering the rest of the spiders' creations had disappeared completely. What if Ben had been too late, they worried. They waited. And waited. And their hearts began to sink, when finally a little black arm poked out through the top of Waverly's cocoon. Only after Waverly reached out for her freedom did the spider silk around her start to melt away. A moment later, Oliver's arm popped out, and his cocoon started to dissolve too. Soon they were both free, looking healthy and strong, if a little damp.

"Are you okay?" Waverly asked Oliver.

"I think so," answered Oliver, getting his bearings. They spoke clearly and easily controlled their bodies. "What about you?"

"I think I'm fine too," replied Waverly. She jumped when she noticed Ramsay kneeling before the throne only a few feet away from them. It took several seconds to convince herself that he was really dead. After the shock of seeing Ramsay wore off, Waverly spotted Ben, and even though he was now a bee, she recognized him instantly. "Ben! Oh Ben, what happened to you?"

The flies shot up to their friend, flying in perfectly straight lines. Ben was still slouched over and lacked the strength to sit up to greet them. But how he smiled at the sight of Waverly and Oliver, so full of life again. "You're alive," Ben said weakly. "I worried I was too late, but you're alive."

"And you're a bee!" said Oliver. "How'd you turn into a bee?"

"I've always been a bee. It's how I became a fly that's the mystery," answered Ben with a tired, half-hearted laugh.

"What happened to your tail?" asked Waverly. "It must hurt. What can we do to help?"

"Waverly, it's no use," Ben said haltingly. "My stinger's been broken off. Bees can't live for long once that happens." A wheezing sound accompanied his labored breaths.

Waverly's and Oliver's eyes filled with tears as the rest of the bugs crowded around the throne. "Don't talk like that," cried Waverly. "You saved us, now maybe we can save you."

"Please don't go," begged Oliver as though he could entice Ben to stay if he only found the right words. "We still have to help you find your home."

"You already did Oliver. This Hive was my home ... many years ago, but I can't stay ... I have to go."

"Then we'll go with you," said Oliver.

"Some day, but for now ... the garden is your home .... Remember, Ramsay's gone .... He has no authority over you ... no power to harm you anymore .... When he died, his curse was broken ... and you were set free .... The whole garden is free."

"You really did it," said Waverly taking Ben's hand. "You saved us." A tear ran down her dimpled cheek.

"I had to," wheezed Ben, taking Oliver's hand too. "I loved you too much not to."

"We love you too," Oliver said softly.

"Stay with me ... a little ... longer." Ben took several short gasps, then Waverly and Oliver felt his hands go limp. They wrapped their arms around him for one final hug and sobbed uncontrollably. They wept because they loved him. They wept because they lost him. Their friend, Ben Beesley, was dead.

***

The other bugs waited, quietly keeping a mournful vigil. When Waverly and Oliver came down from the throne, they were surprised to find so many familiar faces waiting for them. Even though they suffered the effects of the poison during their journey, they remembered all that had happened to them and everyone they met along the way. At first, they were leery of Dap, but the other bugs were quick to vouch for his kindness and bravery. Waverly and Oliver were even more suspicious of Floyd, but nobody jumped to his defense.

"I know you have no good reason to trust me," said Floyd, his natural abrasiveness still apparent no matter how hard he tried to subdue it, "but I have to tell you what happened."

They listened with rapt attention as Floyd told them what had happened in the throne room. He was an experienced liar, and many doubted they were hearing the truth, especially regarding his heroic role in the tale. Still, his rendition of events was plausible—one had only to look at Ramsay and Ben to corroborate the ending.

After Floyd finished his report, the room went quiet. The bugs shifted uncomfortably until Clausewitz said, "There is nothing left to do except give them a proper burial. Ramsay on the Dung Heap, and Ben in a place of honor."

When they were carrying Ramsay to the Dung Heap, Zimra noticed a bite mark, right where Floyd said he got him. With this bit of evidence, everyone was persuaded that Floyd's version of events was not just plausible, but true. When they finished with Ramsay, they went back for Ben and laid him to rest at the entrance to the Hive.

After they said goodbye to Ben, they looked out over the garden and noticed that it had been transformed from something withered and dying into something vibrant and beautiful. The gray pall that hung over them their entire lives had vanished, leaving colors so magnificent they looked as though an entirely new palette had been invented and put on display for the first time. In that moment, the bugs witnessed a garden reborn even as winter closed in.

"I guess Ben freed more than just us bugs from Ramsay's curse," said Meesh. "Look over there!" She pointed to the river, which was flowing again for the first time in years, gushing and churning with an abundance of life-giving water.

The garden's freshly revealed splendor had given them a brief respite from their grief. They took it all in with an intense urgency, as though it would never look so wonderful again.

Eventually, there was nothing left for them to do but go home. Waverly and Oliver gave hugs and heartfelt thanks to the other bugs. When they started to say goodbye, however, Clausewitz interrupted. He insisted on escorting them home, arguing his mission would not be fulfilled until they were safely back in Diterra. Waverly and Oliver accepted and were soon on the road again, this time accompanied by their new friends and headed for home.

This trip could not have been more different from their journey to the Hive. Instead of dangerous jungles, mountains, lakes, and caves, Waverly and Oliver found only a wide path that cut through gently rolling hills. Instead of feeling all alone, they were surrounded by friends. And rather than taking days, it only took a few hours. On the way, they talked about all they had seen and all they had been through, but mostly they talked about Ben.

Their conversation continued uninterrupted until they reached a familiar hill where three little houses made from hollowed-out apples stood, theirs the last one at the top. As Waverly and Oliver raced up the hill, a white creature with six stubby legs and brimming with excitement came sprinting toward them.

"Pupa!" cried Oliver. Pupa jumped on him with such force he knocked Oliver to the ground. His rear wriggled wildly as he licked Oliver's face. Other than being a little cleaner than usual, Pupa was exactly as they left him.

"Thank goodness you're all right," said Todd Lockwood. Todd and Chip stood behind Pupa, looking relieved to see their neighbors again after having sold them out to the spiders. "We took good care of Pupa for you."

"We even gave him a bath," added Chip. "Figured we owed you at least that much."

Waverly and Oliver were stunned. "Thanks," said Oliver, "but I thought Mrs. Galway was looking after him."

"She was," answered Todd, "but you'll never believe what happened. A few hours ago, old lady—I mean, Mrs. Galway walked out of her house with some weird bug. I swear it was a bee!"

"He came over to us, told us he was taking her home, and asked us to watch Pupa until you came back," explained Chip.

"Did the bee tell you his name?" asked Waverly.

"He didn't," said Todd, "but as they were walking away, Mrs. Galway said, 'It's nice to finally see you, Ben.' I think she confused the bee with your friend."

"Where did they go?" asked Oliver.

"They went to the top of the hill," said Todd. "I don't know after that. They just kind of disappeared."

Neither Waverly nor Oliver waited to hear another word and tore up the hill. They saw no sign of Mrs. Galway or the stranger. Indeed, they saw nothing unusual at all until they peeked through the entryway of their house in which two neatly folded jackets with yellow and black stripes had been set next to the back wall.

She picked up a letter that had been placed upon the jackets and read aloud the address on the front: "To My Sister and Brother, Waverly and Oliver Beesley." She smiled, thinking back to the time she called Ben her brother to save him from the spiders. She slid her hand into the envelope, pulled out the letter, and read:

Dear Waverly and Oliver,

I was sorry to leave you so abruptly at the Hive. Although I would like nothing more than to be with you, I had to go away. You know as well as anybody that life takes you where you least expect it. But I miss you dearly, friends, and hope to savor the pleasure of your company again some day.

I must warn you that even though Ramsay's curse over the garden is broken, his spiders will return. They will lose their fear of today. They will come back for vengeance and to claim this garden as their own. The Queen too will come back; the way is prepared for her return. Until then, I need you to stand in my stead. Let the bugs know they need not fear the spiders and no longer have to serve them. After you have told them, show them. Live like you believe it's true.

I have given you both a jacket to wear. When people see you in black and yellow stripes, they will know you are my friends. The spiders will relentlessly harass you, but they can never harm you. If you wear my coat, life will take you places you cannot begin to imagine—all because you belong to me.

It is autumn now, and winter is quickly approaching. Spring feels a long way off, but it will come, and the bees will return for good. When we come, the sun will feel warmer, the colors will be brighter, and the world alto-gether more beautiful than you've ever known it. Until then, wear my coat well.

With great affection, I remain your friend and brother,

Ben Beesley

Waverly folded the letter and placed it back into the envelope. The other bugs had followed them into their house and hung on every word as Waverly read.

She picked up her coat and with one arm in hers already tossed the other jacket to Oliver. He slipped his on over his head. Waverly took one look at Oliver in his bee jacket and suddenly froze. "They all came true," she muttered.

"Huh?" asked Oliver.

"Don't you remember—our wishes from the night we saw the shooting stars? I haven't thought about it since we got bitten, but they all came true. I wished I could bring back something special from Diterra, and we brought Ben home with us. Then you wished to be a bee. And look at you, not only are you wearing a bee's coat, there's a bee who calls you his brother. Then we made a together wish that the spiders would go away, so we'd be free. That happened too, Oliver. It came true. They all came true."

Little did they know it, but the bugs on that hill would have many more strange and amazing adventures. But on that night, they rested. Waverly and Oliver, surrounded by friends, lay flat on their backs looking up at the stars.

"Are you going to make a wish if we see a shooting star?" asked Oliver.

"I've got everything I could possibly want tonight," Waverly answered.

"That's what I was thinking too."

Just then, a streak of yellow light pierced the black sky above. It was a shooting star. Waverly and Oliver both closed their eyes, and at the same time whispered into the night, the gratitude in their hearts finding expression on their lips: "Thank you. Thank you for everything."

Discussion Questions

Chapters 1-4

Comprehension and Recall

1. What were Waverly and Oliver's three wishes? What would you wish for?

2. Why were the Beesleys going to Diterra?

Higher Level Thinking & Personal Response

1. What did the Beesleys do to save the mysterious fly who came out of the hole in the ground? Diterra's motto is "Every Fly For Himself." Why do you think Waverly put herself at risk to help him?

2. Floyd is a mosquito working with the spiders. What does that fact tell you about him? What other things did he do or say that revealed his personality or character?

Chapters 5-8

Comprehension and Recall

1. Why does Ramsay meet with the blind cricket, Croda, every morning? What specific information does Croda share with Ramsay?

2. What was wrong with Waverly and Oliver's neighbor, Mrs. Galway? How did Ben and his friends help her?

3. How did Ramsay come to rule over the garden? In what ways did the garden change once he came to power?

Higher Level Thinking & Personal Response

1. Waverly and Oliver's perception of Mrs. Galway changed. What did they think of her at the beginning of the book and what happened that made them change their mind? Have you ever had a similar experience in which your perception of someone changed? If so, describe the person and what you learned about them that made you think differently of them.

2. Something in Waverly's History Lesson appeared to jog Ben's lost memory. In these early chapters what are some hints or clues as to Ben's origins?

Chapters 9-12

Comprehension and Recall

1. According to Noth, what happens to insects who are bitten by the Malicious Poison Spiders?

2. Why doesn't Waverly want Ben to help her and Oliver after they get bitten by the spiders?

3. When Ben was leading Waverly and Oliver down the mountainside, why did he tie a vine around his waist? Did it accomplish what he thought it would?

Higher Level Thinking & Personal Response

1. When the Beesleys first meet Floyd, what do you, the reader, know about him that they do not? How would they have acted differently if they knew what you knew about Floyd?

2. Von Clausewitz, the fire ant, jailed and threatened the Beesleys, but they helped him any way after he was injured. Do you think they should have helped him or left him on his own? What are some reasons for helping him, or more generally for responding kindly to someone who treats you poorly? What are some reasons for leaving him on his own, or more generally for treating someone in the same manner they treated you?

Chapters 13-16

Comprehension and Recall

1. Why did Waverly and Oliver initially decide to stay in the Mound?

2. Why did Zimra and Ulli, the flies' termite escorts in the Mound, get into an argument? What led Zimra to change her mind?

3. Who were the bugs who helped Ben cross the lake? Why were they at the lake?

Higher Level Thinking & Personal Response

1. Did your impression of the Mound change from the beginning of Chapter 13 to the end of Chapter 14? What details did you observe that suggested it was a less wonderful place than it first appeared?

2. Would you agree that Ben is all alone in trying to save Waverly and Oliver? If yes, in what ways do the Mound and the lake make him feel more isolated and lonely? If no, in what ways has Ben been supported by others in his quest?

3. While on the lake, Ben learns that far more bugs are counting on him than Waverly and Oliver. In what ways does that affect him or his understanding of his mission?

Chapters 17-19

Comprehension and Recall

1. Why was Ben looking for the Keepers of the Light and who did they turn out to be?

2. Where were Waverly and Oliver taken after landing in the spider web at the foot of the Hive?

3. Why did Noth throw Floyd into the spider web with Ben?

4. Who did Ben and Floyd find on the Dung Heap and why were they there?

Higher Level Thinking & Personal Response

1. In what ways have Waverly and Oliver changed from the beginning of the book to when they reached the fireflies' cave? Does knowing what they were like when they were healthy make you view them differently than if you had only been introduced to them as they were when they reached the fireflies' cave? The characters of Waverly and Oliver were based on the author's own children, who have significant special needs and disabilities. Can you think of any kids you might know in real life who are like Waverly and Oliver?

2. Why did the Elders refuse to help Ben? Do you think they did not realize what would happen to Waverly and Oliver if they didn't help, or do you think they just didn't care? In what ways were Zeil and Meesh, who help Ben, different from the Elders?

When we see people struggling in real life, sometimes we react like the Elders and sometimes we act like Zeil and Meesh. Thinking of the people you come in contact with, who among them is struggling and is there anything you can do about it? Is there anything you wish you could for them?

Chapters 20-22

Comprehension and Recall

1. How was Ben able to get away from Ramsay and to the web where Waverly and Oliver were?

2. What changed after Ramsay died and why?

Higher Level Thinking & Personal Response

1. Ramsay is shocked to learn that Ben is actually a bee. Looking back on the book, what clues were there as to Ben's true identity?

2. At the end of the book, Waverly realized all the wishes she made with Oliver came true. In what ways were Croda's prophecies fulfilled?

Made in the USA
Charleston, SC
11 July 2012